A King Production presents…

Rich

or

Famous

Part 3

Love Or Stardom

A Novel

JOY DEJA KING

ISBN 13: 978-0991389056
ISBN 10: 0991389050
Cover concept by Joy Deja King
Cover Model: Joy Deja King

Library of Congress Cataloging-in-Publication Data;
A King Production
Rich Or Famous Part 3/by Joy Deja King
For complete Library of Congress Copyright info visit;
www.joydejaking.com
Twitter @joydejaking

A KING PRODUCTION

A King Production
P.O. Box 912, Collierville, TN 38027

A King Production and the above portrayal logo are trademarks of A King Production LLC

"We found love in a hopeless place."

—Rihanna

This Book is Dedicated To My:

Family, Readers and Supporters.
I LOVE you guys so much. Please believe that!!

—Joy Deja King

Chapter 1

The Only One

Lorenzo stood in deep thought looking out the museum quality insulated glass of his swanky TriBeCa condo. The serene 360-degree panoramic views of Manhattan and the Hudson River couldn't even ease his stress. There were three people dominating his thoughts, one was dead, the other was suffering from memory loss, and the last was over two thousand miles away.

It had been a couple of months, but Lorenzo was still having a difficult time accepting that Carmen was dead. He had been spending time and money trying to figure out who was responsible for her death, but continued to come up empty. Then there was Precious— the only other woman he had ever loved, who hadn't regained her memory since being shot. It bothered Lorenzo that with everything they shared good and bad, Precious didn't remember not one of them. She was now back in love and married to Nico. Then there was Dior, who was the love of his life. Yet he hadn't seen her since they came face to face at the Celebrity Bash for the first time after he found out she faked her death. They had been in communication frequently via phone, but getting a handle on Carmen's death, finding out who was responsible for the shootout at the warehouse that cost Precious her memory, and dealing with Genesis over business, left him no time to get on a plane to LA.

Lorenzo had tried to convince Dior to come to New York, but she was under contract with her new show in LA. They were filming around the clock and she was doing press junkets to promote the upcoming season of the new television series she was in. Lorenzo was thrilled that Dior was finally living her dreams of being famous, but he couldn't help but wonder if he would lose her all over again in the process. Right when Lorenzo was about to pick up his cell phone and call Dior there was a knock at the door interrupting his thoughts.

"Who is it?" he called out heading towards the door.

"Genesis!"

"I should've known," Lorenzo said opening the door. "You're the only person my doorman lets in without calling up first.

"I'm here almost every other day so that's not surprising," Genesis said taking a seat. "Can I get a drink, and if possible make it strong."

"And I thought I was the only one stressed," Lorenzo commented, walking towards his custom-made glass bar that complimented the glass staircase. "I think I better take out the good shit." Lorenzo laughed pouring Genesis a shot of Dalmore 62 Single Highland Malt Scotch.

"Man, I might need the entire bottle if what is rumored to be true turns out to be fact," Genesis huffed before gulping down the shot of scotch in one gulp.

"All the years I've known you, I don't ever

recall seeing you this on edge. What has you so disturbed?" Lorenzo questioned taking a seat across from Genesis.

"I know you weren't around when Talisa got killed." Genesis paused and swallowed hard. He was trying not to get choked up discussing the day his wife died in his arms on their wedding day. "But you know the back story."

"Yes, but everybody who was involved in that is dead. So why..."

"That's what I thought too, but there is a very good chance that I'm wrong," Genesis stated, cutting Lorenzo off before he could finish his thought.

"Well you personally killed CoCo, so we know she's dead. That would only leave..."

"Arnez."

"Didn't you say that your sister's husband Renny killed him?"

"So we thought. But after Renny shot him, he was only concerned about getting Nichelle to the hospital. He didn't wait around to make sure he finished Arnez off, he only assumed he did."

"What makes you think that Renny didn't? This was years ago. Why is this nigga Arnez name ringing bells again now?" Lorenzo wanted to know.

"Because Amir came to me saying that based on some information Aaliyah gave him, he hired an investigator and he came back with the name Arnez."

"Slow down, Genesis. You might be jumpin' the gun. It could be another Arnez or someone impersonating him. There are so many scenarios that are possible. Don't jump to the worst one just yet," Lorenzo advised.

"I want you to be right, but what if Arnez really is alive and he's the one behind all the mayhem we've been going through."

"You talkin' 'bout the shootout at the warehouse that almost cost Precious her life?" Lorenzo asked, leaning in closer.

"Yes," Genesis confirmed nodding his head. "And the shooting at Precious and Nico's wedding.

"Then we need to find out and fast if that motherfucker is still alive. Because if he is, we have to kill him before he kills us. Arnez has caused enough damage and we won't let him cause any more," Lorenzo promised.

Chapter 2

Hollywood Girl

"Wow! This place is amazing!" Dior gushed when she entered the Oviatt Penthouse in Downtown LA for the *Baller Chicks* press junket. "Tony, whoever you all hired to put this shindig together, make sure you keep them on your payroll because this shit right here is officially baller status."

"I'm glad you like it. Max wanted us to go all out for this one. Every major press outlet will be here so we wanted to impress. You can't have a show called *Baller Chicks* and we ain't ballin'," Tony said. Both he and Dior burst out laughing.

"But seriously, I am impressed. This layout is spectacular," Dior stated.

Tony nodded in agreement as he and Dior took the place in.

There was a 12-ton illuminated glass cornice and glass arcade ceiling. Nothing but exquisite Napoleon Marble at every corner and a massive three-faced tower clock with wind chimes. It still retained the art deco style, but it'd been renovated and renovated to its original beauty. It was a divine combination of elegance and grandeur.

"This place is a hidden gem. Who would've thought from the outside that all this fabulousness was going on," Dior continued taking in the ambiance, gourmet appetizers, brunch cooked on site, and full bar with beverage service.

"Hey, Dior. Hey, Tony," the other girls from the show, Bianca, Sherrie, and Destiny said coming over to them.

"This place is super awesome," Bianca stated as the other girls nodded their heads in agreement. "And damn, Dior. I guess you wanted to show everybody who the star is wearing that," Bianca added. Dior wasn't sure if that was an underhanded compliment or a jab. Regardless, one thing was sure, Dior was shining like a star in her all white everything. The cut out, studded, surplice blouse; high waist, tuxedo-striped pants; pumps; and white Chanel bag had understated, sexy, rich, bitch written all over it. Although technically Dior wasn't rich yet, her outfit and demeanor were giving that "I've arrived" vibe.

"Thank you and you all look fabulous too," Dior smirked. Tony decided to usher the ladies over to their seats to do interviews. He wanted this press conference to go smoothly and having a catfight between the leading ladies, was a sure way of guaranteeing that wouldn't happen.

"I'll be over in one second. I have to take this call," Dior said walking off.

"Make it quick," Tony yelled out.

"Hey, Lorenzo. I hope you're calling to let me know you're about to catch that flight and come see me."

"Unfortunately, I can't right now."

"You promised," Dior said disappointed.

"I didn't promise. I told you that I was going to try very hard."

"You've been saying that for the last few

months." Lorenzo could hear the irritation in Dior's voice and he couldn't blame her.

"I know, but things have been so hectic and some new shit has come up. I don't understand why you can't come. Having you all stopped filming?"

"Yeah, but we're doing press rounds for the upcoming season so I can't come right now. I'll see if I have a few days free coming up. I guess a couple days would be better than none."

"Yeah, it would because although I love hearing your sweet voice, I need to see you and feel you again."

"I feel the same way."

"Dior, we need you, now!" Tony walked up behind Dior and whispered in her ear.

"I have to go, but I'll call you later on tonight. I love you, Lorenzo."

"I love you, too."

Hearing those words from Lorenzo always brought a sense of peace and calmness to Dior. It was as if having Lorenzo's love made her more secure even though he wasn't able to be with her. And although Dior wasn't admitting it, was making her resentful. In Dior's mind, she had imagined her and Lorenzo reuniting in this over the top romantic way, but that didn't happen. Since she left New York and came to LA it had only been phone calls and FaceTime. Part of Dior felt like she wasn't a priority for Lorenzo, but she couldn't blame him. She had faked her death and never reached out to him, but Dior thought after they saw each other again at the Celebrity Bash, that they could go right back to the way things were before—when they were in love. So many things had changed since then though. Dior was now on the path to stardom and she wasn't going to let anything stop her, including love.

Chapter 3

Could It Be

Lala sat outside of the one story brick house watching a little girl jump rope. She had been doing this for the last couple of weeks. It took her some time to track Carmen's daughter down, but with a little maneuvering, scheming, research, and a lot of patience she finally did. Lala had even taken pictures of the little girl and had become obsessed with learning all she could since she laid eyes on the child—the day she killed her mother.

Come to find out, the little girl who was named Abigail and called Abby for short, didn't live with Carmen. The little girl lived with Carmen's mother and was raised by her since the day she was born. Lala wasn't certain if the child was Lorenzo's, but she needed to know and decided today would be the day she started getting some answers. Lala didn't believe the little girl saw her face the day she murdered her mother, but to be on the safe side, Lala came prepared in a disguise. With the wig, bifocals, and makeup, Lala's own mother would have a difficult time recognizing her.

"Hello, little girl. Is your mother home?" the child had no idea the woman speaking to her in a sugary sweet voice was her mother's killer.

"My grandmother is in the house," she said as she continued jumping rope.

"Thank you." Lala walked over to the front door and rang the bell. A few seconds later an older woman who had the same dark eyes and hair as Carmen answered.

"Can I help you?" she questioned, peeping her head out the door looking to see what her granddaughter was doing.

"Hello, my name is Tina Clayton," Lala said, flashing a fake business card. "I'm with social services." Through her investigating, Lala was well aware that Carmen's mom was receiving assistance from the government.

"You're not my social worker," she said frowning at Lala.

"I know. I'm with a different department. I was told your regular social worker would be calling to let you know I would be stopping by."

"Nobody called me."

"We've implemented a new program that offers more financial assistance. If you want to call your social worker and set up an appointment that's fine, but I won't have another opening until October."

"That's three months from now. That's okay, come on in," the woman said, welcoming a bigger check if she could get it. Now that Carmen was dead, she didn't have that extra money her daughter provided. Things had been tough financially for her and her granddaughter and the idea of getting a boost in income was exactly what she needed.

"You can have a seat right over here," the woman said. Lala sat down on the sofa and glanced around the living room looking at pictures. There were a lot of Carmen and her granddaughter, but no men except for an older one.

"Now tell me more about this new program."

"First, I need to ask you a few questions."

"Sure go 'head."

Lala crossed her legs and opened up her notebook as if she had a laundry list of questions for the woman, but the paper was blank. "I have to review a few things, but unfortunately your case worker never faxed over all your information. Again, we can wait, but of course that would delay the process further," Lala stated.

"No need for a delay. I'll tell you whatever you need to know."

"Great, that will speed things up. This is an excellent new program and we could all use some additional financial help."

"Ahem. I know I can!" the woman exclaimed.

"Then let's get right to it. Abigail is your granddaughter. How long has she been living with you?"

"Since she was born. At first my daughter was living here too, but when she moved, Abigail stayed with me."

"How old is she?"

"My daughter?"

"No, your granddaughter."

"Oh, she's six."

"Where does your daughter live now?"

There was a long pause before the woman finally spoke. "My daughter..." There was a moment of silence again. "My daughter got killed a few months ago," she said putting her head down.

"I'm so sorry to hear that. My condolences to you and your family." Lala sounded genuinely concerned, even though Carmen's mother was sitting across from her daughter's killer.

"Thank you. It's been hard, but we're managing. If only they would find my daughter's killer. That's the only thing that would give me peace."

"Do the police have any leads?"

"No, and I doubt they are trying very hard," she snapped.

"Why would you say that?"

"Let's just say my daughter wasn't living a very conventional lifestyle. She liked to play with fire, always did. That's why when she decided to move out, I insisted that Abby stay here with me. I didn't have much, but at least I could give the child stability—something Carmen was never capable of."

"What about Abigail's father. Is he in the picture?"

"No, never has been, but at this point in my

life I sure could use his help," the woman admitted, shaking her head.

"Do you have any way of getting in contact with him?"

"Unfortunately, not. Carmen was very secretive about him. I could tell she loved that man though because she was so quick to defend him every time I would say anything bad. But if she loved him so much, I didn't understand why she wouldn't let him be a part of Abby's life. When I would ask, she would say she didn't want to talk about it. I didn't press the issue before, but now that my daughter is no longer here, I plan on finding my granddaughter's father."

"Maybe I can help," Lala offered.

"How?"

"You have been receiving government services. If we can find Abigail's biological father and if he has the means, we can force him to pay child support."

"Even if he doesn't know about Abigail? Because honestly the way my daughter would get so defensive anytime I would question why he had never visited his daughter, my gut was telling me that he didn't know."

"That might be true, but your granddaughter deserves to know her father. If our office can assist you in making that happen, then I would like to help," Lala insisted.

"I could use the help. I have very limited resources. My nephew said that he knew a private investigator that might be able to find him, but every time I call my nephew he says he's waiting for the guy to get back to him. Probably because I don't have any money." She shrugged.

"So you do have some information on the father?" Lala pried.

"Only a picture and his first name."

"You have a picture?" Lala almost couldn't contain her excitement over the revelation.

"Yes. When Carmen was living with me, I caught her one day staring at a picture and she was crying. When I asked her what was wrong, she tried to brush me off and hide the photo, but I grabbed it from her. It was a picture of her and a very nice looking man. I immediately knew he was Abby's father. She looked exactly like him. Carmen tried to deny it at first, but she finally admitted he was Abby's dad."

"You still have the picture?" Lala asked becoming anxious.

"I sure do. Carmen was upset with me because I wouldn't give it back, but I wanted to hold onto it for my granddaughter. One day I wanted to show her the man that was responsible for bringing her into this world."

"Can I see the picture?"

"I don't know how helpful it will be with you finding him."

"Well we have a system in place where we can run photos and see if we can get a match."

"Really?" the woman questioned not seeming totally convinced by what Lala was saying.

"Yes. He might be paying child support to another woman and if so we would have his picture and information on file." Lala was reaching with her lies, but it sounded plausible to her so she ran with it. Plus, Abby's grandmother was an older woman who seemed less than savvy and also very desperate, two things that were working in Lala's favor.

"If it helps," the woman said getting up and walking over to a drawer in the kitchen. "I need this picture back," the woman stated, still holding on to it tightly.

"Of course. When I get back to my office I'll make a copy and bring you back the original," Lala promised.

"Okay, because I'm keeping this picture for my granddaughter. It's the only picture I have of her mother and father together."

"I understand," Lala smiled. *Now give me that damn picture before I rip out your hand old lady*, Lala said to herself continuing to give a fake smile the entire time. The woman seemed reluctant, but finally handed the photo to Lala. "Don't they make a beautiful couple? It's so sad they couldn't have raised Abby as a family. But hopefully you can find him and he can be united with his daughter."

"They do make a beautiful couple." It took all of Lala's strength to say those words. As she stared at the picture her worst fear was confirmed. It was a picture of Carmen and Lorenzo hugged up playfully sitting on top of a car. Lala then turned the picture over and it said Carmen and Lorenzo with a heart in the center. Lala always knew that Carmen was deeply in love with Lorenzo and seeing this photo confirmed it.

Lala did wonder why Carmen never told Lorenzo about their daughter. The only reason she could come up with was that Carmen was too proud and worried she would be rejected by Lorenzo. She didn't want him to think she was trying to trap him with a child. But none of that mattered to Lala because Carmen was no longer a problem and she wanted to make sure that Abigail wouldn't be either.

Chapter 4

Brand New Me

Erick stood on his bedroom terrace that overlooked the garden of his palatial estate. He recently had renovations done on the circular pool that now resembled ancient Roman baths with intricate mosaic tiles and fine marbles. He relished in the detailed craftsmanship on almost a daily basis. Erick admired beautiful things. He had amassed a great fortune and because of that became somewhat of a collector. But with everything he had accumulated, every time Erick stared out at that pool, he was reminded of the one thing he wanted to possess, but was out of his reach.

After all these months, Erick was still having a difficult time accepting that Dior had left him. He figured by now she would've come back. For so long he was the one constant in her life. He had become her crutch in a lot of ways and Erick thought it would always stay that way. He was the one that held her hand throughout her treatment at Rockview Rehabilitation Center. He was the one that introduced her to Tony and was responsible for her big break into the acting world. And he was the one that kept her from going over the edge when she relapsed. Erick felt that he deserved all the credit for everything good in Dior's life and it was killing him that she had moved on and never looked back. He felt completely disrespected by the letter Dior had left him and after reading it, he had decided he no longer wanted her in his life. But that was no longer the case. No matter how hard he tried, Erick couldn't shake his feelings for Dior and he wanted her back.

"Claire, book me a flight to LA," Erick said after calling his assistant.

"Of course, when would you like to leave?"

"As soon as possible. Once you make the reservations, text me with the details," Erick directed before ending the call.

Now that Erick made up his mind that he wanted Dior back, nothing was going to stop him from making it happen.

❀❀❀❀❀❀❀❀❀

"Man, I hope you making magic up in here," Lorenzo said when he entered the studio.

"That's all I make, playboy," Phenomenon shot back from inside the booth, then winked his eye.

The blustering beat and Phenomenon's rapid flow over the base had Lorenzo feeling like they had another hit on their hands. Things were moving very well on the music level for him, so much so that Lorenzo was considering bringing another artist in the fold, but of course he wanted it to be the right person. Although Lorenzo was making moves heavy in the streets he also enjoyed having a legitimate cash flow. He wanted to continue to build that empire and the better he did in the music industry, the more opportunities presented themselves to him.

"My baby sounds good in there, doesn't he?"

Lorenzo turned to see who was talking to him and was surprised to see Courtney sitting over in the cut with one of her girlfriends.

"When did Phenomenon become yo' baby?" Lorenzo chuckled.

"Oh, he didn't tell you?" Courtney smiled.

"Tell me what?"

"Courtney's my girl," Phenomenon yelled over the microphone from the booth, hearing their conversation.

"That's right," Courtney said nodding her head. After cosigning on what Courtney said Phenomenon jumped right back on the track, not missing a beat.

"So when did all this happen?" Lorenzo was curious to know.

"After I appeared in the last video with him, you know, the one you got me."

"Yeah, to get you some shine so you could start paying on that outstanding bill you had wit' me," Lorenzo reminded her.

"True and it worked. I got a ton of video work and I paid you in full," Courtney bragged, feeling proud of herself. Courtney did pay back every cent she owed Lorenzo because he made sure of it. For Lorenzo it wasn't even about the money because it was actually chump change for him. He was pissed for Courtney not only keeping him in the dark about Dior actually being alive, but for her also taking his money for a fraudulent funeral that never took place. He wanted every dollar back that he gave to Courtney, down to the last penny, and he didn't budge.

"No doubt you all caught up," Lorenzo acknowledged.

"Well, I guess I should thank you because Phenomenon and I became cool while shooting the video and kept in touch. One day he asked me out for drinks and we've been kickin' it ever since."

"I see. You've also been discreet."

"We thought it would be best because we wasn't sure what was going to happen between us. But now that we're serious, Phenomenon thought it was time to bring me out."

"So the two of you are serious?" Lorenzo asked, not sounding convinced.

"You heard him say I was his girl. We tried before, but it didn't work out, but I'm not green anymore so I believe we can make it work. You should be happy for us, Lorenzo."

"If my man is happy then I'm happy. Just don't pull no trifling shit wit' him, Courtney, because not only is Phenomenon my artist, but he's also my friend."

"I know I messed up with you over that Dior situation. I made a mistake, but I learned from it. I'm a brand new person, a brand new me. I care about Phenomenon and I don't want to do anything to mess this up."

"Then congrats. I hope things work out for the two of you." Lorenzo might have given Courtney his blessings, but in the back of his mind, all he kept thinking was that she was full of shit. Lorenzo planned on keeping one eye on Courtney because he didn't want her fucking up Phenomenon's life. Lorenzo was well aware of what Courtney was capable of and the verdict was still out on whether or not she had changed for the better.

Chapter 5

Blame Game

When Dior arrived for her fitting, the other girls were already there and had picked out their clothes. They were preparing for a photo shoot to promote the upcoming season. The theme was an opulent, super glamorous look to give the illusion that the women were on Baller Chicks status, which of course was the name of the show.

"Am I late or is everybody else just early," Dior said, when she entered the room.

"You're on time," Theo, the stylist said eyeing his watch.

"We got the time mixed up and got here a little early," Bianca said eyeing the other girls.

"Oh really," Dior commented walking towards the clothes that were hanging up. As she scrolled through the garments hanging up, nothing impressed her. It seemed the other ladies had taken all the good shit because they looked fab.

"Do you see anything you like?" Sherrie questioned with a slight giggle as if she knew what was left to choose from was some bullshit.

"Not really, but I'll make it work," Dior said, reaching for a fuchsia pantsuit. All the outfits were a variation of pinks, but the ladies choices reeked of wealth and sexiness whereas Dior's attire was basically boring.

"I'm sure you will," Destiny chimed in with a sarcastic tone. Dior brushed it off and headed to the bathroom to change into the outfit.

"Who could that be knocking on the door?" Theo asked out loud as he pinned up the hem on Bianca's dress. "Who is it!"

"Tony. Is it okay for me to come in?" he yelled.

"Yes!"

"I didn't want to barge in, in case you ladies were undressed," Tony said as he was coming through the door.

"It's not like you haven't seen some of us naked before," Destiny joked, knowing that Bianca and Tony had a brief fling when she first joined the cast of *Baller Chicks*.

"Love the outfits and you ladies are going to look beautiful in the promo photos and commercials," Tony said ignoring Destiny's playful jab. "Where is Dior? I have something for her."

"Here I am." Dior waved her hand coming out of the bathroom. "How do I look?"

"Beautiful as always, but you're not wearing that," Tony said handing Dior a garment bag.

"What's this?" Dior asked Tony.

"The dress you're wearing for the shoot. Max personally handpicked this for you.

"OMG this is a Zuhair Murad Couture dress! I can't believe I'm wearing this," Dior gasped.

"Why is her dress black?" Bianca popped, smacking the stylist assistant's hand away.

"This is what Max wanted. He felt it would be a great contrast against you ladies in pink," Tony explained.

"You mean it would be a great way to have Dior standout as the star," Bianca snapped becoming heated. "We're all supposed to be equal cast members! When did she become the star of the show?" Bianca was now standing in Tony's face demanding answers.

"Bianca, calm down. Nobody is saying Dior is the star of the show. We're simply going with a different look for the photo shoot. This is an ensemble cast. That hasn't changed."

"Right, Tony. You must've forgotten that I'm not new to this business." Bianca's anger was escalating.

"I haven't forgotten anything. I'm sure you're also aware that Max is our boss. Mine and yours," Tony stressed. He is the one that makes all the final decisions and we will follow them. If for some reason you choose not to then be prepared to deal with the consequences."

"Bianca, I think you are blowing this way out of proportion. It's just a dress," Dior said.

"If you feel that way, Dior, then let me wear it," Bianca countered.

"Well, like Tony said, Max is the boss. If he wants me to wear the dress then I'll wear the dress." Dior smiled. "Now let me go try this on. I'll be back." Dior hurried off to the bathroom with the biggest smile on her face.

"That bitch," Bianca mumbled under her

breath watching in disgust as Dior walked away.

✤✤✤✤✤✤✤✤✤

When Erick arrived in LA he was anxious to get to Dior, but needed to make a quick stop by his condo to shower and change clothes before doing so. He already knew her itinerary for the day and wanted to catch Dior at a dinner the studio was doing for the cast of the show. He wasn't sure how she would react to seeing him after all this time, but Erick was willing to take his chances.

✤✤✤✤✤✤✤✤✤

"Look at her. Do you see the way she's kissing up to Max? I wouldn't be surprised to learn they're fucking," Bianca commented to Sherrie and Destiny while sipping her drink.

"Oh, you think Dior is laying on her back for brownie points the way you laid on yours for Tony," Sherrie mocked.

"Shut up, Sherrie!" Bianca barked.

"They do seem awfully cozy," Destiny added to the conspiracy theory as the girls kept their stares locked on Dior and Max.

"Can you all be anymore obvious," Carla rolled her eyes, walking up on the ladies, catching them off guard.

"Carla, you scared me." Destiny jumped. "Nobody ever told you it's rude to sneak up behind somebody.

"And nobody ever told you it's rude to stare at somebody, especially in a public place. You ladies must work harder at hiding your jealousy. It's not very becoming."

"Oh, please. If anyone should be jealous of Dior it's you, Carla. She did steal your role. Now you're just a side character with limited airtime," Sherrie snarled.

"But unlike the three of you, I'm not jealous. I like Dior. I might not be a regular cast member, but the airtime I do get, has gotten me plenty of work."

"Nobody is jealous of that skank," Bianca spit. "I've been busting my ass for a big break for years and that nobody comes along and wants to take my shine. She doesn't deserve any of this.

"Don't you think you're being a tad bit dramatic, Bianca." Sherrie laughed. "I'm no fan of Dior's, but you can't get mad at her because she's playing the game better than you."

"You mean us because trust we're in this together. It all starts with Dior being positioned to outshine us in the promotional campaign; next they'll be giving her casting authority. When that happens all of our jobs will be in jeopardy."

Bianca's words resonated with the other girls. They couldn't deny that Dior was clearly the higher ups favorite. She did receive the most fan mail and was constantly featured on all the popular blogs. Once Dior joined the cast the ratings did go up which made the show get renewed for another season. It also bruised their egos in the process, knowing that Dior's addition was the reason for the upswing. The girls didn't want Bianca to be right because they needed their jobs.

"So what do you suggest we do?" Destiny was the first to bite.

"Yeah, I'm sure you've already been plotting on how to change things around to work in your favor," Sherrie reasoned.

"I haven't figured it out yet," Bianca revealed, putting emphasis on the word yet. "But in due time. I'm not about to let some ex video girl come in and ruin everything I worked so hard for."

"When you figure it out, just let us know," Sherrie said, looking back over in Dior's and Max's direction.

"Don't worry I will because this will definitely take a group effort. So be ready ladies," Bianca said with a devilish grin.

Chapter 6

We Meet Again

Lorenzo was rushing to get his things together when he heard his doorbell ring. Two things crossed his mind: why didn't his doorman call before letting someone come up and who the fuck would be knocking on his door. He was positive it wasn't Genesis since they had just gotten off the phone and he rarely had visitors. When Lorenzo looked through the peephole he had to do a double take.

"This is a pleasant surprise. What are you doing here? I thought you were on your honeymoon."

"If you let me in, I promise to answer your questions." Precious smiled.

"Of course," Lorenzo laughed. "I apologize. You were the last person I expected to see at my front door so please excuse my rudeness," Lorenzo continued, letting Precious in.

"I almost forgot how beautiful your apartment is," Precious remarked, looking around the over four thousand square feet of open luxury space.

"I wouldn't expect for you to remember. I mean, you did lose your memory," Lorenzo said, gesturing for Precious to have a seat. "Can I get you anything to drink?"

"No, I'm good."

"You certainly look good. I mean that. Marriage suits you."

"I won't be married long," Precious revealed.

"What happened? You and Nico just got married."

Precious hesitated for a minute before responding to what Lorenzo said. "I got my memory back," Precious revealed.

"Are you serious... you remember every-thing?"

"Yes, including our relationship and what we shared."

"It was something special."

"I know. That's why I needed to come see you."

"Precious, when you were in the hospital the only thing I wanted was for you to pull through. I don't pray often enough, but I prayed everyday for your recovery. When you did survive and I realized I was basically a stranger to you, I can't lie, it hurt, deeply. But you were alive and at the end of the day, that's all that really mattered."

"The crazy part is when I lost my memory I had no desire to get it back. I was happy and completely in love with Nico. That was enough for me."

"And now?"

"Now, I want my life back," Precious said. "Are you going somewhere?" she questioned, noticing a suitcase and duffel bag by the staircase.

"As a matter of fact, I am," Lorenzo answered, caught off guard by the question.

"Where? If you don't mind me asking."

"LA."

"For business?"

"Actually I'm going to see Dior."

"So she's alive." Precious stated as if surprised and disappointed.

"It's a long complicated story, but yes, Dior is alive. I guess you really do have your memory back," Lorenzo joked.

"How can I forget that? She was the reason I ended things with you. I didn't want to give my heart to a man that was still carrying a torch for another woman. My ego is much too big for that." Precious smiled. "I'm either first or nothing."

"When we were together you were always first for me."

"I believe that, but I wasn't ready to compete for your affection with a dead woman. But she's not dead at all; she's very much alive."

"You and Dior are the only two women I've ever loved and that will never change."

"Maybe, but you loved her first and she'll always have that edge over any other woman in your life. I know because that's how I feel about Supreme."

"Let me guess, that's the reason you're ending your marriage with Nico."

"Yes. I want Supreme back. The man I was never supposed to get a divorce from in the first place."

"You know there is no love lost between me and Nico, but I feel for the man. This has to be hard on him."

"It is. I mean, I do have love for Nico. We have so much history. I also love you, but my heart is with Supreme. We both made a lot of mistakes in our marriage and I only hope it's not too late to get it back to what it used to be."

"You're an amazing woman and I doubt Supreme has ever stopped loving you."

"You might be right, but we both know that sometimes love isn't enough." Precious sighed. "But listen, I don't want to hold you up. I came over here to get closure. It was important to me to let you know that I do remember and I'll never forget what we shared. You came into my life at a time where I felt lost and with you I found myself again. Thank you for that."

"I should be thanking you. I've never known a woman like you, Precious, and I doubt I ever will. It was an honor to be with you and no matter what happens between you and Supreme, there is not a doubt in my mind you'll come out on top."

"I always loved your confidence in me," Precious said, standing up.

"You make it easy."

"Take care of yourself, Lorenzo, and I hope everything works out between you and Dior. Goodbye." Precious gave Lorenzo a soft kiss on the lips before leaving.

❀❀❀❀❀❀❀❀❀

"Erick! I can't believe you're here!" Dior's eyes widened in delight, seeing the man that had basically changed her life standing in front of her after all these months.

"Yes, I'm here in the flesh. It's good to see you, Dior."

"Don't just stand there, give me a hug, silly!" The two exchanged a long embrace almost forgetting they were in a room full of people. "So what brings you here?"

"The truth? I came here for you."

"I haven't heard from you in months. I assume you got the letter I left for you."

"Yeah, I did. At first I was angry. I didn't understand how you could walk away. I felt we were building something and our bond was strong... I guess I was wrong."

"Erick, it wasn't..."

"Dior, there you are," Tony said interrupting their chat. "Good to see you man." Tony nodded, acknowledging Erick. "I need to steal Dior away for a minute. Max wants to introduce you to some of the shows advertising sponsors."

"Of course. Erick, excuse me for a minute. I'll be back so we can finish this conversation," Dior stated before walking off with Tony.

"She's got this schmoozing thing down pact," Bianca hissed, sliding up next to Erick.

"How are you, Bianca?" Erick seemed less than enthused to see her.

"I seem to be doing better than you."

"Excuse me?" Erick shot Bianca a "what the fuck did you say" glare.

"No need to get upset. You were giving me the lost puppy in love look as Dior walked away. I was concerned."

"Bianca, in all the years I've known you, you've never been concerned about anyone but yourself."

"I know plenty of women that would say the same thing about you. But I didn't come over here to be messy."

"Then why did you come over here?"

"We both want the same thing and I believe we can be beneficial to each other."

"Is that right?" Erick asked, curious to know what Bianca was up to.

"For sure, but of course I don't think this is the right place for us to talk about it. You know my number. Call me tomorrow so we can discuss all the details. If you want Dior back, I advise you not to make me wait because time isn't on your side."

Erick shook his head as Bianca slithered away like the snake she was. By no means was he a fan of hers, but Erick also knew that Bianca could end up helping his cause. He glanced over at Dior. She was wearing a black and gold Michael Costello mini dress with Giuseppe Zanotti bow pump heels. She was laughing and smiling looking every bit the star that she always dreamed of being. It was clear to Erick that Dior was on the path to success and he didn't want her to get there without him.

Chapter 7

Here We Go Again

"Uncle Lorenzo, I'm so happy to see you!" Tania beamed, giving him a hug.

"How's my favorite girl?" Lorenzo picked Tania up and swung her around. Lala watched from a short distance, relishing in the image of seeing her daughter so blissful being in the arms of the man she loved. In Lala's twisted mind, Tania was the only child that Lorenzo needed and if all went well the three of them would finally be a happy family.

"How are you?" Lorenzo said putting Tania back down on the couch and walking over to Lala.

"I'm good. I was glad to get your call that you wanted to come over. Tania has missed you so much."

"I've missed her, too." Lorenzo smiled, watching Tania on the couch playing with her dolls.

"I just cooked some food. Would you like some?" Lala offered.

"I can't. I'm actually on my way to the airport. But I wanted to talk to you before I headed out of town."

"Okay. Let's sit down in the kitchen. Are you sure I can't get you anything?" Lala asked once they were seated.

"I'm straight. But listen, I know I haven't been around a lot lately, but I've been dealing with a lot."

"I know. You're a very busy man and I understand that."

"You and Tania are like family to me and I always want to be a part of her life."

"That's a given, Lorenzo. I don't understand why you would even bring that up."

"I've been meaning to tell you this for a

minute, but it never seemed like the right time."

"Tell me what?" The confusion was written all over Lala's face.

"I'm getting back with Dior."

"What!" Lala's mouth dropped. That was the last thing she was expecting Lorenzo to say. She was aware that Dior was now living in LA for her show and since Lorenzo hadn't mentioned her she figured Dior had left Lorenzo behind for good.

"I know I had said I was letting Dior go, but when I saw her at the Celebrity Bash I realized I was still in love with her."

"Lorenzo, how can you let her suck you back in? Dior is poison. She's brought you nothing but pain. She made you believe she was dead! How could you want to be with a woman that deceitful."

"Lala, I know this is hard for you. So many times I made you believe there was a chance for us and I apologize for that. The last thing I want to do is hurt you, but I didn't want to lead you on. I want to make things work with Dior."

"Is that where you're going... to see Dior?"

Lorenzo put his head down before answering. "Yes, I am."

Lala's eyes watered up and Lorenzo felt

like shit for breaking her heart, but he knew he couldn't put it off any longer.

"Please, don't cry, Lala," he said taking her hand.

"Dior doesn't deserve you. She will hurt you again and again and again. She's selfish! Don't you see that!"

"Keep your voice down. I don't want Tania to think something is wrong."

"But something is wrong. You're leaving the only woman that truly loves you and has your back for an ungrateful, self-centered, wannabe star. You're gonna regret your decision, Lorenzo. I promise you."

"It's my decision and I've made it. I hope in time you'll respect it because I do want you in my life, Lala. You and Tania."

"I would never cut you out of Tania's life. She loves you. She already lost her father. I wouldn't take you away from her too."

"I appreciate that. I hope you don't cut me out of your life either, but I understand if you need time."

"You should go, Lorenzo. I would hate for you to miss your flight," Lala said, getting up from the table. Lala held back her tears as she stayed in the kitchen. She could hear Lorenzo telling Tania goodbye and promising to bring her back a gift from his trip. When she heard the front close and knew Lorenzo was gone, Lala let her tears flow.

❈❈❈❈❈❈❈❈❈❈

"Thanks for letting me give you a ride home," Erick said as he drove Dior back to her condo.

"I think I should be thanking you, especially since my driver for the night decided to disappear on me. I'm tempted to call the car service and report his ass. I've used them several times and they're always so professional. I don't know what happened tonight."

"I might somewhat be to blame," Erick said turning down the volume on the radio.

"Why would you be to blame?"

"I told the driver he was free to go and gave him an extra tip so he wouldn't call and confirm with you that it was okay to do so," Erick admitted.

"So you basically bribed my driver." Dior laughed.

"Pretty much. I'm glad you got a good laugh

out of it." Erick smiled.

"You could've saved yourself some money and just asked me if you could take me home. I would've said yes."

"If only I had been that confident."

"Erick Marquise Dolphin, I thought you invented the word confident," Dior teased. "I'm exaggerating, but you have always been one of the most confident people I've ever met. So I'm surprised you ever doubted yourself."

"For the most part I am confident, but I can't lie and pretend that you didn't shake it a bit when you left me. I've never had a woman leave me before. I always did the leaving."

"Erick, I didn't leave you. I chose to pursue my career."

"Yeah, a career without me being a part of it."

"You didn't want to be a part of it...remember. You basically forbade me from doing the show."

"You know why, Dior." Erick turned towards Dior who was staring out the window.

"But look at me, I'm doing just fine...better than fine. I haven't relapsed or even had the urge to do drugs."

"That's a good thing and I'm happy for you,

but remember you are an addict."

"Would you stop saying that. I'm not an addict. I used to do drugs and I don't anymore, end of story."

"If only sobriety was that cut and dry. Once an addict always an addict, but you can stay clean and I'm glad you have. I'm proud of you and your success. I mean that, Dior."

"That means a lot to me, especially since you're responsible for most of it."

"All I did was give you the opportunity, you put in the work necessary to make it happen. Now that you've shown me that I was wrong..."

"Wait," Dior put her hand up cutting Erick off. "Am I hearing you correctly? Are you admitting that you were wrong and I was right?"

"Yes. I can admit when I'm wrong."

"Okay... proceed with what you were saying."

"You know, I've always believed in your talent, Dior, and I know you can go even further in your career. I would like for you to give me another opportunity to make that happen. You have to admit we always made a great team."

"There's no denying that at one point you were my biggest supporter."

"I still am. We can do this," Erick said, putting his hand on Dior's upper thigh. "I want things back to how they used to be."

"I guess that includes me in your bed."

"Of course. That was the best part." Erick smiled, pressing down on Dior's thigh a little tighter.

"We did share some wonderful times together, Erick, and I'll always be grateful for what you did for me, but a lot of things have changed since then."

"Things like what?"

"Mainly that there can be no us. I can't be back in your bed."

"Why is that?" Erick wanted to know.

"Remember the man Lorenzo I told you about."

"The one who thought you were dead?"

"Yes, him. We reconnected right before I came to LA and we're going to try and make things work."

"Really? So you don't want a future with me so you can rekindle your relationship with a street thug?" Erick's brazen tone pissed Dior off.

"Lorenzo is not a street thug and even if he was, it doesn't automatically make you a better choice than him."

"Listen, Dior..."

"Slow down, you're about to pass my building," Dior said, cutting Erick off. She was now anxious to get out the car so their conversation would be over.

"Dior, I'm sorry. You're right, I was totally out of line for what I just said."

"Aren't you just full of apologies tonight," she commented, giving Erick the side eye.

"I'm serious. I want you to be happy and if Lorenzo makes you happy then I respect that. Even if we can't be together in a romantic way, I would still like for us to do business together."

"I'm not sure if that would be a good idea," Dior said.

"I tell you what, just think about it. Can you do that?"

"I suppose."

"Can you do one more thing for me too?" he asked.

"What's that?" Dior questioned, no longer feeling annoyed with Erick.

"Can you let me walk you to the door?"

"I don't need you to come upstairs with me, Erick."

"Not to your front door, but the building," he clarified.

"Sure."

Erick got out the car quickly and opened the passenger side door before Dior even had a chance to get out. He took her hand as she stepped out and Dior found it cute that Erick was still trying to prove he was the better man for her.

From a distance Lorenzo watched from his car as Dior and some man he had never seen before walked hand and hand together to the building. Rage was brewing inside of him and it took all his strength to control it. His first impulse was to run up on Dior and beat the shit out of the guy who was holding her hand like he was her man, but he stopped himself. But when he saw Dior and the guy start kissing, Lorenzo's rage turned into heartbroken pain. Unable to stomach anymore, Lorenzo sped off, but not before tossing the flowers he got for her out the window. The surprise happy reunion he had envisioned for him and Dior had now turned into an ugly image he wanted to permanently erase from his mind. Lorenzo headed right back to LAX to catch a flight to New York deciding he was done with Dior for good.

Chapter 8

Leading Her On

"We still haven't been able to find Arnez or even confirm that he's alive," Genesis told Lorenzo as they discussed business in his office. "Now we can't seem to locate Aaliyah either. "You know Aaliyah, she's a free spirit so she just might've decided to hop on a plane and go to an island."

"She's young and that's very plausible, but she's also very close to her mother. Precious hasn't heard from her either?"

"No, she hasn't."

"What about her boyfriend... what's his name?" Lorenzo questioned unable to remember his name.

"Dale. We haven't been able to get in touch with him either. We're thinking maybe they're together. Not sure, but we're doing our best to locate her. She doesn't even know that Precious got her memory back."

"Are you worried that her unknown whereabouts has something to do with Arnez?"

"I'm praying that's not the case, but with this life we're in, you never know." Genesis exhaled and stared out his office window that overlooked Central Park.

"Aaliyah is strong. She's a fighter like her mother. She'll be fine. If Arnez or anybody else took her, trust me, they'll be paying us a ransom to give her back. If not, they'll regret the day they ever took her." Lorenzo smiled.

"You're right." Genesis laughed. Both men were trying to find humor in the situation not wanting to believe or think the worse. "So what else is going on? How was your trip to LA?" Genesis asked, wanting to get off the heavy topic of Arnez and Aaliyah.

"Next subject, please." Lorenzo stood up

and poured himself another drink.

"Don't tell me you went all the way to LA and wasn't able to see Dior. I told you not to surprise her. She's a working actress. There's no telling what city or state she might be in at any given time," Genesis reasoned.

"I did get to see Dior but you're right, it probably wasn't the best idea to surprise her. Then again, it gave me the closure I needed."

"Closure... but the two of you just reconnected."

"There won't be any reconnecting. When I showed up she was with another man."

"Lorenzo, man I'm sorry. I know how you were looking forward to making things work with Dior."

"Yeah, but some things aren't meant to be. But listen, there's someplace I need to be. Keep me posted about Aaliyah and Arnez," Lorenzo said reading a text message that just came through from Lala.

"Will do. I'll be in touch," Genesis said, putting his hand on Lorenzo's shoulder. He hated seeing his friend like this. Even though he didn't want to admit it, Genesis knew Lorenzo was in a lot of pain and he hated there was nothing he could do about it.

✺✺✺✺✺✺✺✺✺✺

"Mommy! Mommy! Uncle Lorenzo is here!" Tania screamed when she opened the door and saw him standing there.

"How is the most beautiful little girl in the world?" Lorenzo grinned, lifting Tania up in his arms. She wrapped her little arms around his neck and squeezed extra hard.

"What are you doing here?" Lala gasped, completely shocked.

"In your text you said that Tania really wanted to speak to me so here I am."

"I told you Uncle Lorenzo wouldn't let me down." Tania beamed.

"Never. I'll never let you down. I promise. I also brought you back a gift from my trip." Lorenzo pulled out a brown teddy bear with a pink t-shirt on that said LA Girl. His trip to LA was cut extra short, so he picked it up from the airport before catching his flight back to New York.

"I love it! She's so cute. I'm going to name her Patsy. "

"Why Patsy?" Lala wanted to know.

Tania shrugged her shoulders and said, "I just like the name Patsy." Tania gave Lorenzo another hug and kiss before running upstairs to her bedroom to play with her new bear.

"I still can't believe you're here. You're supposed to be in LA," Lala stated.

"My trip to LA didn't work out."

"Does that mean you didn't go?"

"No, I went."

"Why such a short trip?" Lala needed to know what happened in LA and wasn't going to let up until Lorenzo gave her some answers.

"If you must know, when I showed up I saw Dior with another man."

"What do you mean saw?" she pried, wanting more details.

"She was kissing another man," Lorenzo admitted becoming abrupt.

"Lorenzo, I'm so sorry."

"Are you sure you don't want to say, I told you so, or I knew I was right about her?"

"Of course not. I hate that Dior hurt you again."

"No worries, this was the final and last time."

"Are you sure about that?"

"Positive," Lorenzo said reaching for Lala, pulling her into a kiss. She welcomed his touch again as Lala had believed any chance for a future with Lorenzo was over for good. After a long intense kiss, Lorenzo let Lala go.

"Why are you stopping?"

"Tania's upstairs. I don't want her to come down and see us."

"Let's go to my bedroom."

"I don't think that's a good idea, Lala."

"Yes, it is. I'll take care of Tania and then I'll take care of you. It's almost her bedtime anyway," Lala said, taking Lorenzo's hand and leading him to her bedroom. "You stay here, I'll be right back."

As Lorenzo sat on Lala's bed he knew this didn't feel right, but at the same time he wanted to forget about Dior, if only for a brief moment. She had been consuming every thought each second of the day since he saw Dior in LA and it was driving Lorenzo crazy. There was a sense of familiarity with Lala, which made it easy for Lorenzo to turn to her for comfort. If being with her could ease his pain then he embraced it.

"I'm back," he heard Lala say, shaking Lorenzo out of his thoughts. "Tania is fine and I gave her enough crayons and paper to keep her busy until she falls asleep," she said, locking the bedroom door. "Now, where were we?" Lala gave a seductive smile bending down on the floor in front of Lorenzo. Whatever second thoughts he was having vanished when he felt the warmth of Lala's mouth around his dick. He closed his eyes and laid back on the bed, but Dior's face stayed fixated in his mind.

Chapter 9

Regrets

"Tica, can you please call Tony and let him know that I'm on the way," Dior said staring at herself in the bathroom mirror.

"Sure." Tica stopped packing Dior's suitcase and reached for her cellphone. Tica had only been working as Dior's assistant for less than two weeks, but she had to learn to juggle multiple tasks quickly. If Dior wasn't on set filming, then she was doing a photo shoot, a radio interview, a magazine spread, or hosting an event. She was in demand nonstop and Tica wondered how she ever managed her day before she was hired.

"Hey, Tony. This is Tica. Dior wanted me to let you she is on the way."

"Tell her to hurry. She can't miss this flight," he huffed.

"She won't."

"She better not. Wasn't that the point of hiring you to make sure she showed up for things on time," Tony barked and slammed the phone in Tica's ear.

"Dior, we really have to hurry!" Tica banged on the door in a panicked voice. Although the job didn't pay much, Tica needed the check. Before being hired as Dior's personal assistant, she worked, as a temp but hadn't landed anything permanently. After graduating from college the job offers were nil. When Tony's assistant who also happened to be friends with Tica told her about the job opening she jumped at the opportunity. The pay was crappy, but the perks of going to fabulous parties and being around celebrities appealed to Tica, but being Dior's personal slave and babysitter... not so much.

"Just a minute!" Dior yelled splashing her

face with cold water. Dior hadn't been able to get in touch with Lorenzo and it literally had her sick to her stomach. She grabbed her phone and tried to call him again, but after ringing a couple times it went to voicemail. "WHHHHH-HHHHHHHY!" she belted, slamming her phone down. Lucky for her it didn't break.

"Are you okay in there?" Tica asked becoming worried.

"Just finish packing my clothes and don't worry about me," Dior snapped. She quickly put her hair in a high bun, dabbed on some lip gloss and put on her oversized sunglasses. They had to go to Miami for a few days to film, but the only thing Dior wanted to do was be with Lorenzo. "I'm ready. Let's go," Dior said coming out of the bathroom.

"Great, the car is waiting for us downstairs."

"Then we better go." Dior sighed.

"Tica, I want to apologize for how I spoke to you earlier," Dior said as they sat in the back of the chauffer-driven Escalade. "I have a lot on my mind, but I shouldn't have snapped at you."

"You don't have to apologize, Dior. I know

you're under a lot of pressure. I see your schedule. You're working nonstop. I get stressed just looking at everything you have to do," Tica joked.

"I appreciate you understanding, but my stress has nothing to do with work."

"Then what?"

Dior was reluctant to open up to Tica, but it wasn't as if she had her best friend Brittani sitting in the backseat to listen as she purged her soul. Plus, Dior reasoned, there was no point in having a personal assistant if you couldn't discuss your personal life.

"It's my boyfriend. I mean my ex-boyfriend. I don't know what we are to each other. Right now I feel like I'm nothing to him."

"That can't be true. Any man would be so lucky to have you as a girlfriend. I'm sure you mean a lot to him."

"Then why isn't he taking my calls or responding to my texts?" Dior began to get choked up as if she was about to start crying.

"Dior, don't cry." Tica scooted closer to Dior and stroked her hand. "I'm sure he has a good reason for not being in touch with you. Maybe something happened to him."

"Happened like what?"

"I don't know, but maybe you should find out. Instead of calling have you tried to go see him?"

"He doesn't live here. He lives in New York."

"Last I checked flights go in and out of New York."

"Are you suggesting I catch a flight to New York?"

"You just seem like the type of girl that always finds a way to get what you want. You obviously want your ex so all I'm saying is if you can't get him on the phone, maybe it's time to step your game up. That is, if he's worth it. Only you know the answer to that."

"He's definitely worth it," Dior mumbled as she stared out the passenger window. *Now I just have to figure out how to get to New York without causing Tony to spazz out,* Dior thought to herself as the driver pulled up to the airport.

※※※※※※※※※

"Good morning, love," Lala beamed, holding a tray. "I cooked you breakfast. After last night, I figured you would have a huge appetite."

"It looks delicious," Lorenzo said taking a gulp of the freshly squeezed orange juice.

"You really were incredible last night. Us being together again felt so right."

"It did, but Lala I don't want us to rush things. "

"Why, because you're planning to go back to Dior?"

"No. I'm done with Dior. For good this time."

"Then why can't we be together? I think I've proven my loyalty to you."

"You have and I care about you and Tania very much, but..."

"But you're not over Dior."

"That's not what I was going to say," Lorenzo lied. "Do you think you can get a babysitter tonight?"

"Yes, why?"

"Phenomenon is having a small dinner tonight as his crib and he wanted me to come. I was hoping you would be my date."

"Really?!"

"Yeah, what do you say?"

"Of course. I have to figure out what I should wear. I'll be back." Lala jumped up and ran to her closet.

Lorenzo instantly regretted having sex

with Lala last night, but now he felt obligated to at least try and see if things could work out between them. She had proven her loyalty to him and he adored her daughter. Not only that, part of him felt that he owed her since he was the one that took Darell out of her and Tania's life. Lorenzo promised himself he would give a solid effort to be the man Lala wanted him to be to her and Tania.

※※※※※※※※※

"My man, Lorenzo! I can't believe you showed up." Phenomenon laughed when he opened the door. "Glad you here," he said, smacking Lorenzo's hand.

"I told you I was coming. You know Lala," Lorenzo said, taking her hand, letting her walk in ahead of him.

"Of course I remember Lala. Good to see you." Phenomenon said politely. "I don't think you've ever met my girlfriend, Courtney."

"Hi, I'm Lala."

"Nice to meet you. Come have a seat, I'll get you a drink," Courtney offered, taking Lala into the living room.

"So you with Lala now... what happened to Dior? You went to LA to be with her. I figured she would be your date for tonight."

"Man, we can discuss that later. Where's the food? This is supposed to be a dinner party... right? Where the rest of your guests? I know I can't be early," Lorenzo said looking around.

"I kinda stretched the party part a lil' bit." Phenomenon chuckled, rubbing his hands together.

"Huh?"

"Lorenzo, man, you my only guest. I figured if I told you it was a party, you would feel more obligated to show up."

"So, it's just the four of us?"

"Yep. I wanted you to be the first to know."

"First to know what?"

"I wanted to wait until after dinner to share the good news."

"Phenomenon, would you tell me what the hell is going on."

"We're getting married!" Courtney came running up to them with a big smile on her face and an even bigger rock on her finger. "Phenomenon proposed and I said yes! He wanted you to be the first to know before he announced it to the world," Courtney gushed.

"Yeah man, we're engaged. I'ma be a married man soon." Phenomenon slipped his arm around Courtney's waist giving her a kiss. "This beautiful lady right here is gon' be my wife," he said proudly.

"Babe, this is my mom calling. I can tell her the good news now! I'll be back," Courtney said, skipping off to the bedroom on cloud nine.

"Yo, let me speak to you in private for a minute," Lorenzo said with a stone cold look on his face.

"Sure man." Phenomenon led him to his game/theater room and Lala waited a few minutes before following behind them on the low.

"I guess it would be asking too much to get a congratulations," Phenomenon said as he reached into the mini refrigerator for some Vitamin Water.

"What the hell are you doing man? You gettin' married to this chick... are you serious?"

"You saw that diamond on her finger. That didn't look serious enough for you," he responded sarcastically.

"Tell me why? Why are you in such a rush to get married... is she pregnant? What is it?"

"No, she isn't pregnant. We're in love. Is

that so hard for you to understand?"

"Yeah, sorta. I didn't even know you all were serious. One minute ya' dating the next minute you engaged. What type of shit is that?"

"We were dating for a long time before I even mentioned it to you. We've always clicked and she's living here, why not get married?"

"Because you one of the biggest rappers in the game, you young and now is not the time to be tied down to a chick like Courtney. What else does she do besides music videos? Is that who you really trying to make your wife... some video girl!"

"If anybody would understand I thought it would be you."

"What is that supposed to mean?" Lorenzo snapped.

"When you met Dior, she was a video girl. People warned you about her, but that didn't stop you from falling in love with her."

"Yeah, and I should've listened to those warnings. Dior turned out to be the poison that everybody said she was."

"I guess shit didn't work out with Dior when you went to LA, but that doesn't mean the same will happen for me and Courtney."

"Man, I'm telling you from experience.

Certain types of women are going to be more trouble than what they're worth and Courtney is one of them. I think you too young to be gettin' married, but if you looking for a wife, then settle down wit' a good girl. A woman that can bring you some stability."

"You mean somebody safe like yo' girl, Lala. Come on, Lorenzo. You know you not in love wit' that girl. You feel guilty because you killed Darell. But that shit wasn't yo' fault. Alexus and Brice lied and made you think he was stealing from you. They were some snakes. But running from love because you think a chick like Dior is nothing but trouble, ain't gon' make me give up on what me and Courtney share."

"This conversation ain't about my relationship with Dior or Lala, it's about what's best for you in your personal life and your career. You're my artist on my label and I want what's best for you and marrying shawty ain't it."

"Lorenzo, you know I respect you more than anybody. You one of the main reasons for my career—my success. Not only that but I consider you a friend—a brother."

"I feel the same way about you."

"Then I'm asking you to please respect my decision. Courtney makes me happy and I want her to be my wife. You know in this entertainment shit it's rare to meet someone you feel that gets you; understands your lifestyle and all the bullshit that comes with being a star. And not only that, but you feel comfortable to open up and share your most intimate thoughts. I feel all that with Courtney. I knew she's done some questionable things and her involvement in that Dior situation was fucked up, but she's a good girl. Not the traditional type of good girl, but the right kind for me and that's all that matters."

"Say no more. Congratulations, man," Lorenzo said, giving Phenomenon a hug. The two continued to talk and laugh for a while longer as Lala stood outside the door listening.

All this time I thought Alexus was the one that killed Darell, but it was Lorenzo after all. He was the one who left Tania without her father. But I forgive him because I love Lorenzo. He may not know it yet, but he loves me too and we will be a family. Lorenzo owes us that and so much more, Lala thought to herself.

"Where are Phenomenon and Lorenzo?" Courtney's chipper voice instantly shook Lala out of her deep thoughts.

"Courtney, hey! They're in what I guess you

would call Phenomenon's man cave." Lala joked. "I'm starving. I was just about to go in there and tell them it was time to eat," Lala lied. Playing off her eavesdropping perfectly.

"I'm starving, too. Carrying around this huge rock on my finger has made me work up quite an appetite." Courtney beamed, flinging her hand.

"Your ring is absolutely gorgeous. You're a lucky woman."

"No doubt! I still can't believe I'm going to be the wife of rap superstar Phenomenon."

"You're about to be living millions of girls dreams."

"Sure am, but as long as none of those girls try to make their dreams a reality, they'll be straight because Phenomenon is my man now," Courtney boasted.

"I suggest you keep your man close because you know how thirsty these women out here can be," Lala warned.

"Don't I know it. I guess I should be giving you the same advice. Lorenzo is a major catch. I'm not sure how serious you all are, but you might have some stiff competition."

"I'm assuming you're talking about Dior."

"She is his one true love," Courtney stated

as if a fact.

"Not anymore. He's done with her... for good this time."

"For your sake I hope you're right," Courtney said.

"Don't worry about me. I got this covered." Lala smiled confidently.

Chapter 10

Actin' Up

"Any word on Aaliyah?" Lorenzo questioned as he, Genesis, and Nico sat at a quaint, low-key diner in Harlem to discuss the mounting problems that were causing disarray in their business operation.

"Unfortunately not and I've gone from slightly concerned to outright distraught," Nico revealed.

"So nobody has heard from her?" Lorenzo asked.

"No. The last time I spoke to her was when I was on the plane on my way back from my honeymoon with Precious. I never had a chance to tell her what went down while we were gone. That's not like Aaliyah. She wanted to know why our trip was cut short. Precious hasn't spoken to her and neither has Quentin." Nico shook his head, his face weighed down with worry.

"Amir spoke to her the same day Nico did and he believes Maya might know something, but of course Maya swears she doesn't."

"Do you believe her?" Lorenzo asked Genesis.

"It's hard to say. Quentin swears Maya was with him most of that day and as much as he loves his daughter he wouldn't lie for her when it comes to Aaliyah. We have a couple of our men watching Maya's every move and so far there has been nothing suspicious. She might be innocent."

"And she might not be," Nico interjected.

"True, but she is Quentin's daughter and we can't react unless we have solid proof. If we hurt Maya and end up being wrong about her involvement, the raft of Quentin is something none of us want to deal with."

"You know I have the utmost respect and

love for Quentin. But if I find out that Maya has anything to do with my daughter basically vanishing, nobody will be able to save her, including Quentin. I can promise you."

"Amen to that. I don't know Maya very well, but I do know Aaliyah and of course Precious. She's a good mother and she loves her kids. If Maya is behind this bullshit, I agree she has to be handled, for good this time," Lorenzo added.

"Both of you bring it down a notch. Let's not get ahead of ourselves. We still haven't spoken to her boyfriend Dale. We can't make any decisions about how to proceed until we gather all the facts," Genesis said, trying to be the voice of reason.

"I hear you... so what's the deal with Arnez?" Nico questioned seeing that the back and forth with Genesis was becoming pointless.

"Our men have hit a dead end with him."

"Like literally a dead end? Meaning he really is dead?"

"It's looking that way, Nico. I've had my men digging deep and there is absolutely no trace that Arnez is alive."

"Then if he isn't behind the hit on our organization and family then who the fuck is? This shit is going down as one of the greatest unsolved street mysteries of all time." Nico huffed, pushing away from the table. "I mean damn. How do some motherfuckers keep making moves, but nobody know who the fuck they are. Like they some ghost or some shit."

"I feel you, man. This situation got me on alert too. I hate this uneasy feeling. Lorenzo, you awfully quiet. You care to share your thoughts?" Genesis inquired.

"Is everybody holding?" Lorenzo said so nonchalantly and out the blue that it took Genesis and Nico a second to register his question. "Don't look behind you and continue to act natural," Lorenzo quickly added.

"Yeah, I'm holding." Nico nodded his head agreeing with Genesis.

"Good, because we have some unwanted company," Lorenzo let them know as he eyed the suspicious waiters and a man working behind the cash register. The main thing that caught Lorenzo's eyes was the expensive shoes the waiters were wearing. He owned a pair just like them and knew the exorbitant price. Plus, they seemed too well-groomed to be working as waiters in a hole in the wall diner. "I already sent a text to our men waiting outside that it's about to go down. You boys ready?"

Genesis and Nico both nodded their heads right before all hell broke loose.

⁘⁘⁘⁘⁘⁘⁘⁘⁘

Dior had been persistent in her quest to get in touch with Lorenzo with no luck. During some brief downtime she laid out on the beach contemplating how she could get the hell out of Miami and on a plane to New York.

"Do you feel like having company?" Dior heard someone ask. She lowered her sunglasses and saw Tica standing over her.

"As long as you're not one of the three evil sisters by all means sit down," Dior said, lowering the straps of her bright abstract bikini to avoid tan lines.

"And I thought it was only me who noticed how shady they were towards you," Tica replied, laying down in the folding chaise lounge chair next to Dior.

"I think everybody basically knows. Bianca pretty much flaunts her dislike for me, but the other two try to pretend it's all love. But of course you can only fake the funk for so long. I could care less though. I have a job to do and I'm not going to let those silly gooses stop me from doing it."

"Exactly. Plus everybody knows you're the star of the show. Without you there would be no *Baller Chicks.*"

"Not sure how true that is. I mean yeah, right now I'm the so-called popular character, but one thing I've learned from being in this business is that everybody is replaceable and that includes me."

"Nobody can replace you, Dior. You have that special something. Trust me."

"Thanks, I appreciate you saying that, but honestly, my mind isn't even on this show right now."

"Let me guess, you still haven't been able to get in touch with your ex."

"Nope."

"You need to take the advice I gave you."

"I am! While this hot sun is beaming down on me I'm trying to come up with the perfect excuse to get my ass off this beach and on a flight to New York. I was hoping we would be getting a couple of days off, but it looks like we're working straight through."

"Listen, if you want something bad enough

you'll find a way to make it happen. I'm positive you'll figure it out."

"You're right. We finish shooting our scenes here in a couple of days and then we head back to LA to film some more. Between now and then I will be on a plane to New York."

※※※※※※※※

Lorenzo, Nico, and Genesis each drew their weapons simultaneously, but Lorenzo pulled the trigger of his .40 caliber first sending a hot led ball right at the waiter's chest. The bullet hit him right under his left nipple, dropping him to the ground. He was standing next to the cashier who then reached underneath the counter to retrieve his gun, but Nico was able bust off as the bullet ripped through the skin of his neck. The man grabbed his throat as blood gushed out, drenching his hands. He gasped for air, but nothing but more blood drizzled from his mouth. The other two waiters began shooting wildly as Nico, Genesis, and Lorenzo ducked and took cover under the tables.

"Watch out!" Genesis barked to Nico as one

of the waiters snuck up behind sending a bullet in Nico's direction. Genesis was able to move Nico out the way and fire off two shots hitting the guy in his lower arm and leg.

Then out of nowhere a slew of goons came charging from the back with weapons raised. But they showed up a moment too late because Lorenzo, Genesis, and Nico's men descended on the diner clutching their AR-15s and blasting each assailant one at a time. The bodies began dropping one after another until it looked like a blood bath.

"Is everybody straight?" Lorenzo called out when silence finally lingered in the air.

"We good," Genesis said as he stood up and then Nico.

"Man, I'm gettin' too old for this shit," Nico grumbled, rubbing his head.

"You and me both," Genesis chimed in.

"We can't think about none of that shit right now. Somebody is out for our blood bad and if we don't find them soon, they might succeed on their next try. For me, that's unacceptable. It's time we make some major moves and I know exactly where we should start," Lorenzo said as the three men walked out of the diner, leaving the dead bodies behind.

Chapter 11

Closer

"Mr. Taylor, there is a Dior here to see you." When Lorenzo heard his doorman say that Dior was there, his emotions were mixed. He had been avoiding all her calls since he made a surprise visit to LA and saw her kissing another man. He got right back on a flight, never giving her an opportunity to explain who the man was and part of him wanted to keep it that way.

"Mr. Taylor, are you still there?" the doorman questioned after the long silence.

"Yeah, I'm here. Don't let her come up. Tell her I'm not available."

"I'm sorry Miss, but Mr. Taylor is unavailable," the doorman informed Dior after hanging up with Lorenzo.

"What do you mean he's unavailable? Was that him on the phone?"

"All I can say is that I can't let you go up. Enjoy the rest of your afternoon." He smiled.

"Listen," Dior said taking off her sunglasses. "I don't know what's going on with Lorenzo, but I really need to see him. Please let..."

"Wait!" the doorman said suddenly standing up from his chair. Dior moved back, perplexed by the man's sudden movement and the expression on his face. "Aren't you the girl on that show *Baller Chicks*?"

"Yes, I am."

"My wife and daughter love that show! They make me watch it with them every week. If I have to work that night, they record it so I can see it when I get home. We're even watching reruns until the new season starts. I thought you looked familiar, but didn't recognize you until you took off the sunglasses. Wait until I tell my wife and daughter! They'll never believe me! We really are fans!"

"Thank you." Dior smiled. "Let them know the new season starts in a couple of months." Dior was trying to be extra polite, but all she really wanted to do was get on the elevator so she could go see Lorenzo.

"Can I ask you a huge favor?"

"Sure, what is it?"

"Will you take a picture with me? That's the only way they'll believe I'm telling the truth about seeing you."

"Sure, I can do that. But only if you do something for me."

"I already know what it is and you got it." He winked. Before Dior could say another word, the doorman had his phone out and they were having a mini photo shoot right there in the building lobby.

I guess being on a popular television show did have its perks, Dior thought to herself as the elevator headed to the top floor.

When the elevator doors opened to Lorenzo's floor, Dior had butterflies in her stomach. He hadn't been taking her calls and she knew it wasn't by accident. They hadn't spoken in weeks and now he was having his doorman turn her away. Dior wondered if he was with another woman and maybe that was the reason he wouldn't let her up. All Dior knew was she was determined to find out what was going on.

Dior knocked on the door and then started banging when Lorenzo was taking too long to answer. "Answer the door, Lorenzo!" Dior yelled as she continued to pound on the door.

"What do you want?" were the words out of Lorenzo's mouth when he opened the door.

"I've been on a flight for hours and then in a taxi stuck in traffic for I don't know how long and all you can say to me is what do you want? What the hell is going on with you, Lorenzo?"

"I didn't ask you to do all that," he replied nonchalantly.

"I did it because you weren't taking my calls or texts and I missed you. I wanted to see you."

"Is that right?" Lorenzo's tone was condescending and dismissive.

"What the fuck is up with you! We haven't seen each other since the Celebrity Bash and you're treating me like shit. Was all this a game to you, some sort of payback for me faking my death? I thought we were past that, but I guess I was wrong. You pretended to still be in love with me and wanted to try again to make our relationship work so you could break my heart."

"Wow! Those acting classes are really paying off," Lorenzo said, clapping his hands as if giving Dior a standing ovation. "Should we cue the tears?"

"Fuck you, Lorenzo! I won't let you to do this to me again."

"Do what? Not fall for your bullshit."

"Bullshit... what are you talking about?"

"I saw you, Dior."

"Saw me where?"

"With your tongue down some nigga's throat." Dior's face frowned up as she struggled to figure out what Lorenzo was talking about. "You can stop trying to come up with a lie to explain what I saw."

"What you saw... hold on a minute. How..."

"I was in LA," Lorenzo belted, cutting Dior off.

"When were you in LA?"

"It doesn't matter. The point is, you've been keeping yourself very busy without me. So cut all this bullshit about you missing me. You've been over there in Hollywood living your life and doing exactly what the fuck you want. So get the hell away from my front door!" After ripping into Dior, Lorenzo turned to slam the door shut.

"Lorenzo, please, I can explain!" Dior called

out, putting her hand up to keep the door from closing.

"Save it! I don't want to hear shit you have to say."

"That was Erick. It was a kiss goodbye. I told him you have my heart and it's true," Dior wailed, doing her best to convince Lorenzo not to walk away.

Her assertion stopped Lorenzo in his tracks. But his back was still facing Dior.

"It's true. He came to LA and showed up at a dinner the show was having. My driver for the night disappeared and Erick gave me a ride home. He walked me to my building and asked could he come up, but I wouldn't let him. He then kissed me and yes I kissed him back, but it was a kiss letting Erick know it was really over. You have to believe me, Lorenzo."

"There's always something with you, Dior." Lorenzo shook his head still not turning to face her.

"Okay, maybe I shouldn't have reciprocated the kiss, but if I wanted Erick I would be with him. I'm here begging to be with you. We've been through so much and it took us too long to find our way back to each other. Don't let it end now. Not like this," Dior said, reaching for

Lorenzo's hand. This time he didn't turn her away instead he took Dior in his arms.

"I can't shake you no matter how hard I try," Lorenzo said gazing into Dior's eyes.

"Stop trying. I'm alive and you're not in jail. We've survived and are lucky enough to have a second chance at love. Let's embrace it."

Lorenzo didn't say another word, instead he closed his front door, lifted Dior up, and carried her upstairs to his bedroom.

Lorenzo placed Dior down on the bed and no words needed to be spoken between them. Instead their eyes did all of the talking. Lorenzo was the first to begin undressing and Dior instantly wanted to come out of her lace panties when she saw his ripped body. She had never forgotten how chiseled to perfection he was, but seeing him in the flesh had Dior all caught up in her sexual feelings.

Lorenzo was equally if not more aroused. He couldn't stop staring at Dior as she got up from the bed and stood in front of him. Although her body was covered in a wrap dress, it seemed as if her curves wanted to push through the silk fabric. Unable to contain his lust any longer, Lorenzo pulled the strap on the dress causing it to unravel. It opened revealing Dior's voluptuous physique. Lorenzo couldn't help but admire Dior's beauty. Before unclasping her lace bra he took a moment to stare as his dick hardened by simply imagining how good it was going to feel being inside of her.

Lorenzo wrapped his hands around Dior's waist and pulled her body up against his. Her body wilted in his arms, as if she was beginning to melt.

"You have no idea how long I've dreamed of this moment," Dior said softly, yearning for their bodies to unite. Lorenzo placed his finger on Dior's mouth as if telling her not to say another word. He then replaced his finger with the warmth of his lips that instantly made Dior's pussy wet.

Lorenzo gently pushed Dior onto the bed, before climbing on top of her. The tip of his dick massaged the outside of her now dripping wet clit. He slid half of his dick inside of her, making Dior moan lightly and almost giving her an orgasm before getting off a full stroke.

Dior grabbed onto Lorenzo's lower back and pulled his body closer, shoving the rest of his dick inside of her. Her moans turned into grunts as she tried to take it all in, but couldn't, even though her juices were flowing. As she tried to back up off of it, Lorenzo chased her up the bed until there was nowhere else for her to go. With each thrust, the pain began to turn into pleasure. She wrapped her legs around his and dug her nails into his back while biting his shoulder. In the mist of their intense lovemaking, Dior couldn't believe that she had been without Lorenzo for this long and promised herself it would never happen again.

Chapter 12

Ain't Nobody

"I wish we could lay together like this for the rest of our lives." Dior smiled. She loved waking up with Lorenzo's strong arms wrapped around her. It brought back those feelings of love and security that only he was able to give her.

"I don't know about forever, but we can at least stay like this for the next week or so," Lorenzo said moving Dior's hair so he could kiss her earlobe.

"That sounds perfect. Only if we could make it happen."

"Why can't we? I might have to step out a few times to handle some business, but for the most part I'll be up under you." Lorenzo was now kissing on Dior's neck making it almost impossible for her to talk. She was becoming aroused again, even though they had been making love off and on all night and morning.

"I cancelled my taping yesterday saying I had a family emergency. I have to get back today," Dior mumbled as she turned over so Lorenzo could slide back inside her. "One more time and then I really have to go," she promised herself.

※※※※※※※※※

"So is the queen showing up for work today or is she going to cancel again," Bianca snarled while getting her makeup done.

"Well, Tony made her call time to later this afternoon so she has plenty of time to get here," Sherrie said, while the finishing touches were made to her hair.

"Of course Tony gave her an afternoon call time. He always makes exceptions for her." Bianca rolled her eyes.

"Don't be jealous. I know you miss Tony making exceptions for you. Oh, how quickly things change." Sherrie giggled. Destiny tried to hold back her laughter, but couldn't resist. Even the stylist doing hair and makeup had to join in.

"Whatever. I'm not jealous," Bianca sighed as she picked up a fashion magazine and flipped through it as if unbothered. "The point is, Dior shouldn't be getting preferential treatment."

"To be fair, it was a family emergency," Destiny conceded.

"I didn't know Dior even had family. Isn't she like an orphan or something." Everyone in the room glanced over at Bianca. They weren't sure if she was making a tasteless joke or if she was being sincerely mean spirited.

Bianca wasn't paying a soul in the room any attention. She could care less what they thought about her. Her only interest was getting rid of the competition and securing what she thought was her rightful spot as the star of the show. Bianca had already placed a call to Erick and was waiting for him to get back to her. She felt the rest of the ladies were too weak and silly to be any real help to her. To bring Dior down she felt she needed a real backer like Erick. The only glitch was that Erick was still in love with her adversary so Bianca knew she had to play her cards right so he would feel like they were both winning. If she wasn't able to convince him of that, Bianca was sure that Erick wouldn't agree to help her cause.

❀❀❀❀❀❀❀❀❀

"I hate to see you go," Lorenzo said between kisses as he and Dior rode down the elevator to the lobby of his building.

"Does that mean you'll be coming to LA soon?" Dior smiled before nuzzling the tip of Lorenzo's nose.

"Baby, I'ma try to get all my business handled as quickly as possible so I can come be with you. I have a couple of serious issues that require my personal attention, but when I'm done with them I'm all yours."

"You promise?"

"You know I don't like to make promises, but for you... I promise. I don't want to let you go now. I don't know why you won't let me take you to the airport."

"It will be much easier and faster if I just get in a cab. Plus, if I let you drive me to the airport, I'm afraid I'll never get on my flight," Dior said, laying her head on Lorenzo's shoulder.

As Dior and Lorenzo kissed and held hands, the two lovebirds were oblivious to Lala and Tania watching them. Mother and child were walking across the street, but stopped in their tracks at the sight of them.

"Mommy, who is that woman Uncle Lorenzo is holding hands with?" Tania questioned. "Uncle Lo—!" Lala quickly put her hand over Tania's mouth and rushed her behind the building so they wouldn't be seen or heard.

"Tania, keep your voice down," Lala said sternly, but in a low tone.

"I thought we were supposed to be surprising Uncle Lorenzo and bringing him lunch," Tania said with wide eyes. Lala looked down at the carefully wrapped plates of home cook meal she had prepared for them. She then peeked her head around and watched as Lorenzo and Dior kissed lovingly before she got in a cab. Lala felt as if her whole world had come crashing down on her in a blink of an eye.

This bitch will just not go away! How in the hell did she worm her way back into Lorenzo's life? He said he was done with her for good this time and I believed him! Lorenzo belongs with me. I'm the only woman for him. He knows it too, but Dior always finds a way to slither her way back into his life. I won't let her destroy our happy family. She doesn't deserve Lorenzo and I will make sure he knows it once and for all, 'cause ain't nobody gon' have Lorenzo but me, Lala thought to herself as she waited for Lorenzo to go back inside of his building before getting back in her car with Tania and driving off.

Chapter 13

Backseat

"I'm back bitches," Dior beamed when she arrived on set. "I know you all were so worried about me and wanted to make sure that I was able to come in for work. You all can now relax, I'm here, but I do appreciate your concern." She smiled as Bianca, Sherrie and Destiny looked as if they wanted to barf.

"I was worried about you. So glad you're here. How is everything with your family?" Tony asked giving Dior a hug.

"I was able to take care of everything. My family is good now and so am I. Thank you, Tony for giving me the day off. Who knew you could get so much accomplished in twenty-four hours. But now that I have resolved my family emergency, I'm ready to get back to work."

"Wonderful! They're waiting for you in hair and makeup. Go get glammed and we'll see you on the set shortly."

Once Dior had left the scene, Bianca made a beeline straight to Tony. "You know her story about a family emergency was a bunch of bullshit," she spit.

"And good afternoon to you too, Bianca," Tony said walking off.

"Don't walk away from me. Last time I checked, you're not the type of man that likes to be played."

"Who exactly is playing me, Bianca? You?"

"Me? I'm trying to save your ass. Dior is full of herself. I'm sure if you do a little investigating you will find out that whatever little emergency had nothing to do with family. What if she was off doing a secret audition for another show? Wouldn't you feel awfully stupid that you were the one that gave her the time off to make it happen?"

"Bianca, jealousy does not look good on you. The only person that should feel stupid right now is you. Why are you so concerned about what Dior is doing with her day off? What you need to be concerned with is running your lines so we don't have to keep reshooting your scenes."

"Fine, Tony, have it your way, but don't say I didn't warn you." Bianca was seething after her encounter with Tony. On top of that Erick wasn't returning her phone calls so she decided it was time to take matters into her own hands. If nobody wanted to assist her with taking down Dior then she would do it herself.

❁❁❁❁❁❁❁❁❁❁

"Thank you for meeting with me so soon."

"You said it was an emergency and the money you were talking sounded right."

"It is and you will be well compensated."

"I'm sure you're a woman of your word, but I'm gonna need you to show me the money."

Lala eyed the man sitting across from her. They had met at the ferry in Staten Island. He was supposed to be excellent at what he did so Lala was willing to cough up the cash to motivate him to get the job done. He was a below average looking Italian guy that didn't even seem capable of wrecking havoc on anybody's life, but his resume said otherwise. Lala took the white envelope from her purse and handed it over. The man took his time counting his money making sure she wasn't a dollar short.

"Continue," he finally said after being satisfied that his money was in order.

Lala handed him two photos, one with Dior's picture on top. "I need you to find out everything you can about this woman, but most importantly what's going on in her life right now. Once you do, I'll tell you how to proceed."

The man nodded his head, "And this one?" he questioned looking at the second picture.

"I want her dead."

"Are you sure?"

"Positive. The sooner the better."

"Once I begin there is no pressing pause. So be sure what you're asking because I will deliver."

"I'm positive. I want you to deliver and if you do so quickly, I'll add a nice bonus to what I've already given you."

"Then I'll be in touch very soon."

The man went off in his direction and Lala enjoyed the boat ride. She smiled and gloated at the thought that soon her competition would be eliminated and she would have Lorenzo all to herself.

❋❋❋❋❋❋❋❋❋

"Nigga, you stay in some shit. I can't believe they came at you like that at that spot in Harlem. Glad you straight. I need you for that meeting with the label tomorrow," Phenomenon cracked as he and Lorenzo kicked back in his theater room. "Nah, you know I would be fucked up if anything happened to you."

"You ain't got to tell me. But I do gotta be careful out here. I haven't even had my first seed yet. Ain't no way I'm leaving this earth without procreating."

"Man, I feel you on that. Is that your way of tellin' me you 'bout to make a baby with Lala?"

"Nope."

"Well then who? I haven't heard you mention no other contenders or are you just making plans for the future?" Phenomenon questioned.

"Actually, I'm back with Dior."

"I knew that shit was gon' happen!" Phenomenon jumped up and said as if he had just scored the winning shot in the NBA finals. "You tried to play so hard like you was done wit' homegirl, but Dior got yo' heart. Always has and always will. You need to just admit that shit and stop playing."

"You right."

"Huh? Say that again, I don't think I heard you," Phenomenon teased, putting his hand behind his ear and leaning forward.

"I said you're right. She came to see me a few days ago. It was all a big misunderstanding and we worked things out. I love that girl. I really do."

"I know you do. Your entire face light up when you say her name, even when you mad at her. The two of you belong together. I always knew that."

"I didn't want to admit it, but you're right. Dior will always have my heart so we might as well make it work. I wish she didn't have to leave so soon, but Hollywood calls."

"That's the only thing I see being an issue for the two of you. I don't know if you'll be able to handle her having to put her career first."

"Why does her career have to come first?"

"Lorenzo, you know how this entertainment shit work. If Dior wants to be a huge star, which I'm sure she does, it's going to require making her career her number one priority. Can you handle being number two?"

"This must be some sort of trick question." Lorenzo frowned, leaning back in the recliner chair.

"Nah, I'm just keepin' it all the way real. The fact that Courtney doesn't really have anything going on but me makes our relationship perfect. If I want her on tour she can be right there on the road wit' me. If I'm working late in the studio, she can chill there too. The point is, her only real obligation is to me. Dior is officially in the game now and her star is only going to be rising. I hope you can deal wit' that."

"Everything you're saying is true, but Dior and I have been through a lot and we'll get through this too. She's wanted this fame shit for so long and I'm not gonna get in the way of that. I support her one hundred percent. If that means I have to take the backseat sometimes then so be it."

"I knew you loved that girl! I'm proud

of you, man." Phenomenon laughed, patting Lorenzo on the back.

Lorenzo had never even contemplated that he would have to take a backseat to Dior's career. He then quickly remembered that when she came to visit she had to turn right around and head back to LA for work. For the last few months it had been impossible for them to see each other because business kept him in New York and work obligations kept Dior in LA. So Phenomenon had made valid points that he had never considered until now. But none of that mattered because Lorenzo made up his mind that he was committed to Dior and that was that on that.

Chapter 14

Complications

"Courtney, thanks so much for the invite to lunch. I can't remember the last time I had a girl's day out." Lala smiled, taking a sip of her water.

"I thought you might need it. I mean every time we talk on the phone, you're either on mommy duty, cooking, or cleaning."

"I agree. I do need to loosen up a bit."

"Exactly. Every girl deserves to have some

fun. Like maybe you should put the water down and have some wine like I am," Courtney suggested, sipping down the last of her Moscato before refilling her glass.

"Well, let me get some food in my stomach first."

"Whatever you order, you'll love. The food here is delicious. But I have to admit I'm surprised you have an appetite. I thought I was going to have to force you to eat."

"Why would you think that?" Lala questioned baffled by Courtney's comment.

"I'm sure you're devastated that Lorenzo went back to Dior. I know I wouldn't have an appetite if Phenomenon left me for his ex." After taking another gulp of her wine, Courtney looked up at Lala who was silent. "OMG, you don't know. Fuck! Lorenzo hasn't told you yet?"

"No. How did you find out? I guess Phenomenon told you?"

"He didn't exactly tell me. The other day Lorenzo was at the house and I overheard them talking. He told Phenomenon he was back with Dior. I can't say I was surprised. I tried to warn you, Lala, but you seemed convinced he was done with her. I'm so sorry you had to find out like this... from me. I thought for sure Lorenzo would've come clean."

"No, he hasn't. I guess he's trying to figure out how to break the news to me," Lala said calmly. After that day Lala spotted Lorenzo and Dior walking out of his building, hand in hand, she had spoken to him a few times, but he never mentioned they were back together. She could tell he was trying to avoid seeing her face-to-face and figured it was out of guilt.

"Probably so, but he needs to come clean with you. Please don't tell him that I opened my mouth and spilled the tea. He already can't stand my ass. I don't need to give him another reason to talk shit about me to Phenomenon."

"I won't. But why does Lorenzo dislike you?"

"Oh, he never told you. Girl, I lied to him, but it was only to protect Dior. She had a really bad drug problem and when he got arrested Dior did have a major setback. She needed to go to rehab and thought faking her death was the only way to do it."

"Seems a bit extreme."

"Well, Dior is an actress so being dramatic comes with the territory."

"Are the two of you still friends?"

"Not really. I mean, I'm super happy for her

and all her success, but we kinda lost touch after she went to rehab. It's like Dior wanted a fresh start. But it's a small world because my friend Tica who I went to school with is now Dior's assistant."

"Really?"

"Yes! Isn't that wild." Courtney giggled getting a kick out of the crazy coincidence.

"It really is."

"But I told her not to mention to Dior that we were friends. Dior probably wouldn't care, but Tica really needs the job and she just got it so I wouldn't want her to take any chances of messing that up."

"I feel you. That probably is for the best."

"So what are you going to do about Lorenzo?"

"I guess I have to wait it out. I mean, you never know what can happen. Lorenzo might not be able to handle a long distance relationship and decide it's best if he works things out with me."

"Damn Lala, I have to admire your determination. Lorenzo is a great catch, but not sure if he's worth waiting on for the rest of your life."

"Trust me, I have no intentions of waiting on Lorenzo for the rest of my life and I won't have to. Dior is not the woman for him, I am. He'll see. Now let's order our food because I'm starving."

Courtney was tipsy, but not so drunk that she couldn't help feeling that Lala's attitude about her relationship with Lorenzo seemed off. She wasn't able to put her finger on it, but Courtney thought that Lala seemed a little too sure of herself. But as she sipped on her fourth glass of wine, Courtney threw caution to the wind and figured it was just the liquor making her so suspicious.

❖❖❖❖❖❖❖❖❖

"That's a wrap!" the director said after Dior finished her scene.

"Thank goodness because I am so out of here." Dior had been on set all day and part of the night. She was exhausted to the point that she didn't even bother removing her makeup or changing her clothes. She grabbed her duffel bag, purse, and headed to her car.

"Leaving so soon," Bianca stepped in front of Dior and said, as she was about to walk out the door.

"Umm yeah, that's what it looks like right," Dior smacked. Ready to push Bianca out of her way.

"Can you hold up for a minute? I really wanted to speak to you about something."

"Can't this wait until tomorrow? I'm beat and honestly you're the last person I want to talk to right now. Now excuse me." Dior brushed past Bianca anxious to get to her car. Running into Bianca made her bad mood even worse, but when she looked down at her cell and saw Lorenzo calling that all changed.

"Hey, baby. I got the biggest smile on my face when I saw you calling."

"Good, 'cause you got me over here smiling too, but hearing your voice does that to me."

"Stop it, you're making me blush, Lorenzo."

"I need to be doing more than that and I will very soon."

"Does that mean you're coming to LA?"

"You know I don't break any promises. I'll be there in a couple of days. I have a label meeting tomorrow for Phenomenon then the next day I'm on a plane to see you."

"Baby, I can't wait. You're exactly what I need right now."

"I feel the same way. What are you about to do now?"

"On my way home... finally. I've been on set all day and the only thing I want to do is have a glass of wine and crawl into bed. If I was coming home to you, that would make my night perfect."

"Soon. We'll be together soon. But listen, I have to go inside and handle some business. Call me before you go to bed, okay?"

"Will do. I love you." Lorenzo could hear Dior smiling through the phone when she said those words.

"I love you too, babe."

Dior hit the unlock button and got into her car. She blasted "Now & Forever" by Drake and opened the sunroof to make sure she didn't fall asleep. Dior knew with how drained she was she should've called a car service to take her home, but she didn't feel like waiting. She wanted to get off set, out of the building, and into her own car ASAP.

As Dior pulled out the parking garage, she turned left onto the main street and headed towards the highway. The next song didn't even have a chance to come on when a dark colored minivan came out of nowhere and slammed into the back of Dior's car.

"What the fuck!" Dior yelled out, caught completely off guard. She wanted to get out the car and curse the motherfucker out who hit her, but it was dark and there was barely any traffic. Dior didn't want to take a chance the driver could do more than just fuck her car up. She decided to dial 911 instead and get some backup in case she was dealing with a nut. But before she could even make the call, the driver slammed into her again, this time even harder. Now Dior was frantic. It was obvious this wasn't an accident. Whoever was behind the wheel was slamming into her car on purpose. She pressed down on her gas trying to put some distance between herself and the minivan.

"Thank goodness!" Dior sighed in relief when it seemed she had lost the driver. She continued on her route home for a couple more minutes until another car pulled up beside her. The car was darkly tinted and Dior couldn't even see a shadow of who was inside. When she sped up the car stayed behind, so Dior relaxed and thought nothing of it. Then a few seconds later the car began to rush towards her, but before Dior could try to get away the car crashed directly on the driver side door, completely running her off the road. It all happened so fast that Dior's body flung back then forward causing the airbag to release and knocking her out.

※※※※※※※※※※

"It's been months now and you're no closer to finding out who is responsible for killing Carmen. Man, you gotta give me something," Lorenzo said to Ace as they sat across from each other at their usual meeting spot in the Bronx. Lorenzo had been using Ace's services for years and typically by now, he would've had some leads for Lorenzo, but he had been coming up empty for months.

"Lorenzo, this ain't like me, but this shit got me stumped. It's like nobody knows nothing. I've talked to everybody that I think might know something, but they know nothing. Carmen kept her shit close to the vest. She did a lot of dirt for you, but nobody said Carmen had any enemies so it doesn't seem like anybody knew what she was doing. I can't find a motive."

"I hear you, Ace, but clearly somebody had

a motive. Ain't nobody just walking into her crib, putting bullets in her body for no fuckin' reason."

"I don't know. Maybe it had something to do with her daughter. A pissed off baby daddy. But he seems to be a ghost because I can't even get a name on him," Ace said, putting his beer down on top of the bar.

"Daughter? Carmen didn't have a daughter."

"Yes, she did. The little girl is about six or seven."

"You must be mistaken. I've never seen Carmen pregnant or with a child. She's never even mentioned she had a child. Carmen wouldn't keep something like that from me."

"Listen, I know for a fact Carmen has a daughter."

"Why are you just telling me this?"

"I didn't think it was a big fuckin' deal. She's a woman and I'm sure she wan't no virgin. If you have sex you make babies. Plus, I figured you knew." Ace shrugged.

"So you think Carmen's daughter had something to do with her murder?"

"I don't know. I'm just grasping for straws at this point. This shit baffling the fuck out of me."

"Where is Carmen's daughter?" Lorenzo asked, unable to get the revelation that Carmen had a child out of his mind.

"From what I understand she lives with Carmen's mother. She's the one that raised the little girl."

"That makes sense. It's probably why I never saw her, but it still doesn't explain why Carmen never told me about her. Keep searching for Carmen's killer, but I want you to find out everything you can about her daughter and I also want to know who the father is."

"No problem. I'll get on it right away."

"Good, because if she has some crazy baby daddy that killed her, then that nigga need to be dealt with. I also wanna make sure her child is financially straight because Carmen's daughter will want for nothing. I'll make sure of that."

Chapter 15

Numb

"Where am I?" Dior mumbled as she slowly opened her eyes.

"You're in the hospital," the nurse informed Dior who had been heavily medicated.

"What happened... how did I end up here?"

"You were in a bad car accident. But you're going to be okay," the nurse assured Dior.

Flashes of what happened the night before began flooding Dior's mind. She remembered getting hit by a minivan and then another car running her off the road. Dior had no recollection of what happened after that.

"Did the police catch the driver who ran me off the road?"

"Unfortunately not. By the time the police arrived your car was the only one there. The police do want to interview you. Are you up to talking to them right now or do you want to wait until the medicine wears off?"

"No, I'll talk to them now or whenever they're ready."

"Okay, I'll let them know. But take it easy. You were pretty banged up and you really need to get your rest," the nurse insisted.

"What time is it?"

"Two o'clock."

"In the afternoon!" Dior raised up quickly and instantly felt excruciating pain shoot through her back. "I have to get out of here. I was supposed to be on set five hours ago!" her voice flustered.

"Miss, you're not going anywhere," the nurse rushed to Dior's side to calm her down. Did you not understand what I said? You were in a serious car accident. You're going to be in the hospital for at least a couple of days, maybe longer."

"Like hell I am! I have to get to work. They're expecting me on set. We're already behind. I can't miss any days." Dior began to get hysterical.

"I need you to calm down," the nurse insisted, but Dior wasn't listening. She seemed to be having a major meltdown as if out of her mind. The nurse didn't hesitate to give Dior a sedative, thinking it was for the best due to her irrational behavior.

"I have to get out of here... I have to get out of here..." Dior kept saying over and over again until the sedative kicked in and she fell back into a deep sleep.

※※※※※※※※※

"Lorenzo, this is nice, us having dinner. We haven't had any quality alone time lately. I know business has been crazy for you lately, but I'm glad you were able to make time for me," Lala said sweetly. Lala was doing an excellent job of pretending she had no clue he was back with Dior.

"Things have been crazy. Between business and finding out who killed Carmen, I can't seem to get a break."

"You still haven't made any progress with finding Carmen's killer?"

"No, but we might have a slight lead. Come to find out Carmen had a daughter. I had no idea."

"Really? What does her daughter have to do with her death?"

"Maybe nothing or maybe everything. The guy working on this for me said that maybe she had a falling out with her daughter's father and he killed her. It might be far-fetched but worth looking into. Hopefully when we find out who the father of Carmen's daughter is we will find her killer."

"For your sake I hope so. I know Carmen was a good friend of yours."

"Yeah, I hope so. I want to put closure on this. I feel like I owe Carmen that. But this situation isn't why I asked you to have dinner with me tonight," Lorenzo said, sliding his plate to the side and placing his folded hands on the table.

"This sounds serious. Are you going to ask Tania and me to move in with you? If so, the answer is yes! You know how much Tania loves you. You're the closest person she has to a father, especially since Alexus took Darell away from us. Sometimes I still can't believe he's gone. Darell loved and respected you so much, Lorenzo. But I'm sure he's smiling down on us, knowing you've stepped up to the plate and are filling his shoes."

Lala was laying it on extra thick. Now that she knew Lorenzo was really the one that pulled the trigger and killed Darell, she wanted to use that information to make him feel as guilty as possible. As cool, calm, and collected as Lorenzo always appeared she could almost feel him squirming in his seat.

"Darell was a good man," Lorenzo finally managed to say.

"He was more than that... he was loyal to you until the very end. For Alexus to kill him like that is unforgivable. But justice was served. Alexus is dead and Darell's death did bring us closer together."

"It did bring us together and Tania. I love that little girl so much."

"I know you do and she loves you too. I think it's wonderful we're finally going to be a real family."

Lorenzo looked up at Lala. The candlelight was illuminating against her face. Her hair was down cascading around her shoulders. The peach colored lace dress she was wearing made her appear so innocent and fragile and that was no accident. Lala knew Lorenzo asked her to dinner to drop the Dior bomb on her and she wanted to make it as difficult for him as possible.

"Lala, I've already made it clear that you and Tania will always be family to me. I have love for both of you."

"I know and..."

"Let me finish," Lorenzo said not wanting Lala to interrupt him. "I need to say this. "

"Say what?"

"I knew this would be difficult, but not this difficult. There is no easy way to say it. I'm back with Dior."

"What! You said you were done with her for good this time. Why would you get back with her?"

"I know what I said and at the time I meant it. But I made a mistake and I was wrong. Dior came to see me and explained what really happened."

"I'll never understand why you continue to take Dior back. She'll only disappoint you again. But it's your life, Lorenzo. I wish you the best."

Lorenzo was stunned at how well Lala was taking the news. It made him feel even guiltier for ending his relationship with Lala before it even had a chance to really start again.

"I wasn't expecting you to make this so easy."

"I guess I've become so used to you leaving me for Dior that I've become somewhat numb to it."

"It's not like that. I..."

"No need to explain, Lorenzo, I've heard it all before. Although I wish you well, I haven't changed my mind about Dior. Your relationship with her is never going to work. She'll always choose fame and stardom over you. So I'm not worried because you'll be back. You always do," Lala said before getting up from the table and leaving Lorenzo sitting there alone. He watched as Lala exited the restaurant and couldn't help but wonder if she was right.

The moment Lala was out of Lorenzo's sight she reached in her purse to retrieve her cell phone. She couldn't place the call fast enough.

"It's a little late to be calling me, don't you think?"

"With the amount of money I'm paying you, you need to be available to take my call twenty four seven."

"What can I do for you?" the man asked, not even trying to hide the fact he was irritated that Lala was calling him this late on a Friday night, even if she was a high-paying client.

"I need you to move faster on both jobs I hired you for."

"How fast are you talking?"

"For the first person I need that done like yesterday."

"That will require me to bring someone else in and it's going to cost you extra."

"Fine, I'll pay extra just get it done!" Lala snapped and ended her call.

Lala may have played it cool with Lorenzo, but she was more determined than ever to have Lorenzo to herself and nothing or no one was going to stop her.

❦❦❦❦❦❦❦❦❦

"Can you believe that Dior is late for work? This girl is something else. Who does she think she is," Sherrie smacked to Destiny and Bianca during a break from filming.

"I'm not surprised. This is Dior's world, remember, we're just props," Destiny added.

"Bianca, I can't believe you're not raising hell. When has it been okay with you for Queen Bee to be tardy," Sherrie popped.

"It's not okay. I think everyone is well aware how I feel about Miss Dior."

"I'm glad you ladies are all here together." Tony's unexpected sudden entrance made the women jump.

"Are you okay? You seem anxious," Sherrie commented.

"No, I'm not okay. Dior was in a horrible car accident last night after she left here."

"What!" the ladies said in unison.

"She's in the hospital and it doesn't look good."

"What do you mean? Is she going to die?" Bianca questioned.

"No, it's not that serious, but she will be in the hospital for the next few days which is going to ruin our shooting schedule since Dior is basically in every scene.

"So what are you going to do about the shooting schedule?" Destiny wanted to know.

"I don't know yet, but I'll figure it out. But we're wrapping things up for the day, so you ladies can go," Tony informed them.

"There's no need to shut down shooting because of Dior," Bianca jumped up and bawled.

"Like I said, Dior is in just about every scene. I'll need to speak with the writers of the show to figure out how to adjust some things. I'm also going to see Dior at the hospital so I can get a better idea of just how long she'll be unable to work. Until then, I'm shutting things down. I'll be in touch with you ladies."

The three women stared at each other not pleased with what Tony had just told them. It was one thing for them to make jokes about Dior being the star of the show, but having shit shut down due to her absence made it abundantly clear she was and none of them liked that. Bianca couldn't stand there any longer. She got up and rushed after Tony.

"Tony wait!" she called out as he was halfway down the hall.

"What is it, Bianca?"

"I think you're making a mistake," Bianca said when she reached Tony. "You can write Dior's absence into the show and then maybe bring Carla in to take her place while she's out and then expand our roles," Bianca suggested.

"That's an interesting suggestion and it

might work and it might not. I'll take it into consideration, but I need to see Dior first before I make any decisions. But I'll think about what you said."

"Thanks, Tony!" Bianca was grinning from ear to ear as she walked away from Tony and headed back to the other ladies.

"You seem to be in a much better mood than you were before you ran out of this room," Destiny said. "I assume you ran off to talk to Tony."

"Yep."

"What did he say that put a smile on your face?" Sherrie asked.

"He said he would consider my idea of writing Dior's absence into the show, expanding our roles, and having Carla replace Dior temporarily." Although Bianca was secretly hoping Carla would be a more permanent replacement.

"Tony said that!" both and Destiny and Sherrie were surprised Tony would even consider making the change since he seemed to be Dior's biggest fan.

"Yes, he did. Tony is a businessman. He's going to do what's best for the show and if that means moving on without Dior then that's what he'll do." Bianca smiled.

Chapter 16

Crazy Meet Crazy

Lorenzo and Phenomenon waited patiently for their meeting to begin. They were sitting down with the record label executives to discuss the promotion for Phenomenon's last album and to get an idea what sort of deal they would be putting on the table for a new recording contract. Normally, Phenomenon didn't move without at least three members of his entourage, but Lorenzo had already schooled him that this was official business shit and they had to conduct themselves as such.

"Hi, can I get you all anything?" a lady came in and asked them as they started to become a little restless.

"You can get this meeting started," Lorenzo stated.

"We apologize for the delay. There have been a few changes at the label recently so we want to make sure we have the correct people in the meeting. Everyone should be here short-ly. Again, we apologize. Are you sure I can't get you all anything while you're waiting?"

"Positive but thanks," Lorenzo said before looking over at Phenomenon. "Changes, correct people... what type of shit they got going on over here?" Lorenzo said to Phenomenon after the lady left.

"I have no idea."

"Something don't feel right to me."

"Lorenzo, relax. I'm one of the biggest and best-selling acts on the label. I don't give a damn what changes they made, money is money and I'm a moneymaker," Phenomenon stated lean-ing back in his chair like he didn't have a con-cern in the world.

"Gentlemen, we apologize for the delay, but

it's a pleasure to meet both of you. I'm Robert Anderson, but you can call me Rob," a tall lanky white guy said with an inviting yet fake smile. They all shook hands as three other men came in that Lorenzo and Phenomenon had never seen before.

"When the lady said changes I didn't realize it would entail an entire new staff." Lorenzo made eye contact with the unfamiliar faces, sizing each up.

"Yes. Recently the label was bought out and there are some new owners. The main one is Mr. Dolphin, who is here today to sit in on the meeting."

"Lorenzo, Phenomenon, it's a pleasure to meet you both. I'm sure everyone here is ready to get this meeting started. Let's do that," Mr. Dolphin said. "I'll let Clay, who oversees your department, begin."

"As we're all aware, Phenomenon, this is your final album on the label before your contract is up and if you're interested, we would like to re-sign you for a new three album deal."

"Of course I'm interested." Phenomeon smiled. This place has been like home for me and I want us to continue to do big things together... even bigger things."

"I agree," Lorenzo began. "We have some ideas that we think will not only take Phenomenon to an even higher status, but also be beneficial to the label. We have a couple of artists that we recently signed to my label. Phenomenon is about to go on tour and both will open for him and we'll have them do some features on a few of Phenomenon's songs before they drop their own singles. Since of course our music is distributed through you all, that's more money for you," Lorenzo explained.

"New talent is always something we're interested in and—"

"Hold on for a minute, Clay," Mr. Dolphin said, cutting him off. "Before we begin discussing Phenomenon's future albums and other artists, let's present our offer to him."

"Sounds good. Show me the money," Phenomenon said, rubbing his hands together. Mr. Dolphin slid over an envelope. Lorenzo opened it first and then handed it over to Phenomenon.

"What do you think?" Mr. Dolphin questioned.

"I think this is some sort of joke! Unless this is just a bonus on top of the money you offering for a new record deal? Let me see those numbers. If not, it's missing several zeroes."

Phenomenon slid the envelope back over to Mr. Dolphin.

"We think this is a fair offer based on the economical climate of music."

"Nigga, that's some bullshit! I'm one of the few rappers that's still selling records. Get the fuck outta here!"

"Relax," Lorenzo said to Phenomenon touching his shoulder. "I got this. Mr. Dolphin, we both know that numbers don't lie. I'm sure before you became one of the buyers of this label you and your attorney did a very thorough examination of sales. With that being said, we're all aware that Phenomenon's have risen with each new release and his next CD is on track to have one of the biggest first week sales this year."

"All that is true, but record sales as a whole are still on the decline and in order for a company to stay in business and make a profit we have to be more conservative with the advances we give to artists and the marketing budget we provide. It's just business."

"You're right. It's just business so we'll be declining your offer," Lorenzo said ready for the meeting to be over.

"That's unfortunate. If Phenomenon won't

be continuing on with the label then you leave us no choice but to put a limited amount of money in marketing his upcoming album. We need to reserve our budget for artists that will be part of this company for the long haul."

"So you gon' purposely try to sabotage my next album so my sales won't be shit and won't no other label step up and give me the mother-fuckin' money I deserve!" Phenomenon barked before standing up and kicking over the chair next to him. "You backstabbing bastards fuckin' wit' the wrong nigga. I tear this whole fuckin' office up and drag each of you in it while I'm doin' it!" he threatened.

"Stop... now," Lorenzo said those two words calmly and quietly to Phenomenon, but from the look on his face he didn't need to say anything else. Phenomenon was still breathing hard and you could damn near see flames coming from his head, but he sat back down and didn't say another word.

"Gentlemen, clearly this meeting is over," Lorenzo stood up and said. "What's your name again?" Lorenzo looked across the table and asked.

"Dolphin... Erick Dolphin."

"Mr. Dolphin, it was a pleasure meeting you

and I'll be in touch."

"Pleasure my ass," Phenomenon spit when they walked out the glass double doors. "I can't believe them motherfuckers tried to play me like that. All that fuckin' money I done made that company. What type of business was that shit. Unloyal bastards."

"That wasn't business that was personal," Lorenzo stated getting on his phone. "I need you to find out everything you can about a Erick Dolphin. I need the information ASAP!" he said before ending the call. Lorenzo had been in the game long enough to know when something had nothing to do with business and was all personal. Erick Dolphin clearly had a hard on for him and Phenomenon. Lorenzo wanted to know why.

❊❊❊❊❊❊❊❊❊

"Courtney, I'm so glad you answered. I've been trying to get in touch with you for a few days now."

"Hey, Tica!" I apologize but I've been a little hectic. Phenomenon is about to go on tour and

I'll be on the road with him."

"Sounds exciting."

"Yeah, but it was so last minute so I'm try-ing to squeeze getting three weeks of stuff done in three days."

"I hear you. That sounds like my life on a daily basis being Dior's assistant."

"How is that going?"

"It's coming, but I stay busy. Then Dior was in a horrible car accident the other night so everybody is going crazy, especially her. She's ready to get back to work, but she's also in a lot of pain. She's taking so much pain medicine I'm starting to get a little concerned."

"You should be!" Courtney blurted.

"I was only joking," Tica quickly said.

"Well, it's not a joke. You don't know?"

"Know what?"

"Dior had a serious drug problem. She went to rehab and everything," Courtney disclosed.

"Oh wow, I had no idea."

"Make sure you keep an eye on her. I may not talk to Dior anymore, but she really does have a good heart. I would hate for her to start using again."

"I will, but I wasn't calling you about Dior."

"What's up then?"

"I got a message from this woman who said that she got my number from you."

"What woman?"

"Her name is Lala."

"Lala? Have you spoken with her?"

"No, not yet. I wanted to ask you about her first."

"Don't talk to her, Tica."

"If you don't want me speaking to her then why did you give her my phone number?"

"I never gave Lala your number. She lied!"

"Why would she do that?"

"Whatever the reason she's up to no good and I'm sure it has to do with Dior. When we went to lunch a couple of weeks ago I mentioned that you were Dior's personal assistant. Never did I think she would track you down. I don't know what she's up to, but I'm going to get to the bottom of it. But seriously, Tica stay away from her. Something is off with that girl."

"I'm glad I called you and thanks for the warning."

"No problem. But listen, I have to go. We'll talk soon." The second Courtney got off the phone with Tica she called Lala.

"Hey, Courtney what's up?" Lala answered sounding sweet and chipper.

"I need to see you."

"I'm home right now. You wanna stop by?"

"Sure, I'm on my way over. I'll see you in a little bit." Courtney didn't even bother to finish packing. She hung up with Lala, grabbed her purse, car keys, and headed out.

❈❈❈❈❈❈❈❈❈

"Dior, I'm so glad you're okay. When Tica told me you were in a car accident and then the hospital I was so worried."

"I'm just glad you're here, Brittani. Thank God for Tica. After the car accident my phone got missing. When Tica showed up for work and I was MIA she began calling around everywhere looking for me. Thank goodness she had enough sense to try hospitals too. She got in touch with Tony, but I really need for her to get in touch with Lorenzo. I don't know his number by heart or anybody's number for that matter."

"Calm down, Dior."

"How can I calm down? He was supposed to come to LA to see me. I'm sure he's been trying to call me, but he can't. We just got back on track and the last thing I need him to think is that I'm being shady. Fuck!!!"

"Did you back up your contacts to iCloud?"

"Hell no! But Tica is supposed to get me a new phone today with the same number so hopefully Lorenzo will call me. I really need him right now and I'm so ready to get out of this fuckin' hospital!"

"Is everything okay in here?" a nurse came in and asked. "I heard some yelling. I wanted to make sure everything is okay."

"No, everything is not okay. I'm in a lot of pain. I need some more pain medicine."

"The chart says you were just given some medicine an hour ago. It's too soon to give you another dosage."

"Too soon? I'm in fuckin' excruciating pain and it's too soon for you to give me some medicine? Why the hell am I in the hospital if you all can't make the pain go away!" Dior screamed.

"Let me go speak to your doctor," the nurse said, refusing to get into a screaming match with her patient.

"Forget it... just forget! I don't need my doctor. I need to get the hell out of this place."

"Dior, you have to calm down. Getting upset isn't good for you. I hate seeing you like this,"

Brittani said sadly.

"My back hurts so much!" Dior exclaimed, almost in tears. Dior reached for a piece of paper on the stand next to her and picked up the room phone.

"Who are you calling?" Brittani asked.

"Tica."

"Hello," Tica answered.

"Hey, it's me Dior."

"Hey, Dior. I'm getting your phone now."

"Great, but when you come can you bring me some more candy. My back is killing me."

"Sure, I'm on it. See you shortly. Do you want me to bring you anything else?"

"No, that's it, but hurry," Dior said before hanging up. "Tica has been so heaven sent. They knew what they were doing when they created personal assistants."

"I'm assuming candy is code word for painkillers."

"Duh!" Dior rolled her eyes.

"We both know your history, Dior. I understand you've been in a terrible accident and you're in a lot of pain, but please be careful. I don't want you having a relapse."

"I know, Brittani, but a girl has to do what a girl has to do. Tony came to see me the other day and of course the three witches are plotting on how to use my accident as a way to get me off the show."

"Dior, Tony loves you. He's not going to let you off the show."

"Out of sight, out of mind. They're running a business over there and one monkey is not going to stop the show! I have to get better soon so I can get back to work and if taking some painkillers will speed this shit up then so be it. Thank goodness there wasn't any noticeable injury on my face or body."

"You've worked so hard to get where you're at now and I know you don't want it to be taken away, but your health is more important than any amount of fame."

"I hear you, Brittani, but let me worry about my health. I love you and I appreciate your friendship, but I can handle this. I'll be back to work before you know it and before those three bitches can start planning my farewell party."

❊❊❊❊❊❊❊❊❊❊

"When you said you were coming right over

you meant it." Lala smiled when she opened the door for Courtney.

"This couldn't wait." Courtney rushed past Lala brushing against her arm. "Is your daughter here? I don't want her to hear any of this."

"No. Tania is with my mother. I'm home alone." Lala smiled. "Can I get you something to drink... maybe some wine? I know how much you like to drink."

"I don't want any wine and you can wipe that smirk off your face because this isn't a friendly visit."

"Courtney, what's wrong? I thought we were friends?"

"Friends don't lie on other friends."

"I don't understand. I never lied on you."

"You called my friend Tica and left her a message saying that I gave you her number. That's a lie."

"I apologize. I didn't think it was a big deal and technically I didn't lie. I did get her number from you.

"I never gave you Tica's number."

"That day we had lunch and you were in a drunken stupor. You left your phone on the table when you went to the restroom. To my surprise I didn't need a code to unlock it."

"You went through my phone!" Courtney popped, astounded by Lala's admission.

"I just wanted to ask her some questions. I don't understand why you're making such a big deal out of this."

"I knew something was a little off about you, but I'm starting to believe you might be unstable."

"Courtney, I think you need to calm down."

"Calm down! You went through my phone and got my friend's number without my permission and then called her. The only questions you could've had for Tica were about Dior."

"So what if I wanted to ask her some questions about Dior. Although Lorenzo and I aren't together anymore I still consider him a friend and I'm very protective of him. I want to make sure Dior doesn't hurt him again."

"So you track down Dior's assistant. Oh please! But you know what, you can explain all this to Lorenzo yourself."

"What are you saying?"

"What I'm saying is that I will be telling Lorenzo that you called my friend trying to get information about Dior. Let's see if he believes this bullshit explanation you're giving. Because frankly, I think you're lying. I think you're up to a lot more than what you are admitting and if anybody will dissect and figure this shit out, it's Lorenzo. When it comes to his precious Dior, he is relentless. I should know because when Lorenzo figured out my lies he was willing to see me dead to get the truth from me."

"I can't let you tell Lorenzo, Courtney. That will ruin all my plans. Everything I've worked so hard to make happen. Please don't do that," Lala pleaded.

"All what plans? Never mind. I'm tired of listening to your lies! Save it for Lorenzo." As Courtney turned to walk away, with swiftness Lala reached for a vase on the table, striking her over the head. Courtney's body slumped to the floor. Lala raised the vase to strike her again, but quickly changed her mind."

"I don't need any more blood on this floor to clean up," Lala said talking to herself out loud. Courtney had been knocked out cold but she wasn't dead... yet. That would soon change. Lala began dragging Courtney's limp body towards the garage and placed her in the trunk of her car.

Lala drove far out to a remote location and put two bullets in Courtney's head before rolling her dead body down a steep hill. She had no remorse for killing a girl who had only tried to be her friend. But when it came to Lala's quest of having Lorenzo to herself, nobody was going to stop her and that included Courtney.

Chapter 17

Allure

"I know you're so happy to be home." Brittani smiled as her and Dior sat outside on her balcony that overlooked the pool.

"You know it, but I'm happier that I'll be back to work tomorrow. I'm also excited about going to this party tonight. I feel like I haven't worn any decent clothes in forever."

"Well, you were in the hospital for an extended period of time and you've been home for less than a week."

"It will be nice to get dressed up, put some makeup on, and feel sexy again. I wish you were able to come with me tonight to the party."

"Girl, I've been here for over a week. I need to get back home."

"I know. I appreciate you staying with me all this time. You truly are a great friend. I wish you could be here with me all the time. You need to move yo' ass to LA!"

"I don't think I can do that, but I will be back in a few weeks for the awards show. It's so exciting you were nominated for best new actress. I'm so happy for you, Dior."

"Thank you! I still can't believe I was nominated. This should at least secure me a spot on the next season of *Baller Chicks*."

"Dior, with all the great things that are happening for you, I hate that you're always so worried about your job security. That show is lucky to have you. You're like a breath of fresh air when you come across the screen. I wish you knew how special you are."

"It means a lot to me to hear you say that, but this business is so cutthroat. Honestly, Brittani, if I didn't love what I did so much the pressure would be unbearable. But I'm built for this. All my dreams of becoming rich and famous are starting to happen now if only I could have love too."

"You still haven't talked to Lorenzo?"

"Nope, he hasn't called yet and of course I have no way of getting in touch with him. I miss him so much. I just hope he's okay."

"Don't worry about Lorenzo, he's fine, trust me. You just focus on yourself. I love you so much. I don't want anything to happen to you."

"I love you too, Brittani. I'm so lucky to have you as a best friend." The two women held each other tightly. Dior did feel lucky to have Brittani in her life, but that didn't stop her heart from craving Lorenzo.

❦❦❦❦❦❦❦❦❦❦

"Lorenzo, I don't know what the fuck is going on! It's as if Courtney has vanished. Man, I'm going crazy," Phenomenon muttered, pacing back and forth on his living room floor.

"Phenomenon, we're going to find her."

"When! She's been missing for a fuckin' week. The only thing I have is a text message from her saying she has to make a stop, but she'll be home in a couple of hours. They find her car in some parking lot, but then all traces of her disappear. Something happened to her, Lorenzo, something bad."

"Don't think like that. You have to stay positive." Lorenzo was trying his best to sound optimistic, but deep down he was worried like a motherfucker. He was no fan of Courtney, but he also believed that she did love Phenomenon and wouldn't up and leave him. He had his people trying to track her down, but they were coming up empty just like they did with Carmen. He was still waiting for them to give him information on Carmen's daughter and Erick Dolphin. He was beginning to think it was time for him to hire some new private investigators.

"It's hard to stay positive when my gut is tellin' me something different. I'm supposed to be on the road right now. My tour opens tomorrow, but I'm here in my crib in New York."

"So what do you want to do? Do you want to postpone the tour?"

"Yeah, I do, but I know I need to do this tour especially since my label ain't gon' do shit to promote me. Sorry fucks! This tour is my way to keep my fan base hyped. My new CD drops next month. I need that shit to do good."

"And it will, Phenomenon. I've already hired a marketing company to do the shit the label should be doing."

"You did? That's gon' cost you a fortune."

"Man, you worth it. You think I'm gon' let them snake motherfuckers stop what we created. I'll never let that shit happen. This type of bullshit is the exact reason why I haven't given up my street hustle. I got more than enough money to get the word out properly that Phenomenon is here and here to stay. You feel me?"

"I do feel you and I ain't gon' let you down. You've done so much for my career and me. I will be in Philly tomorrow to kick off my tour."

"Phenomenon, you don't have to do that. If you're not ready to start your tour then we can wait. We'll figure it out."

"Nah, I won't let that happen. You're right, we did create some pretty amazing shit and I ain't gon' let nobody fuck that shit up neither. Forget about having one of the biggest first week sales this year, I'm gonna have the best!"

"That's what I'm talkin' 'bout. You go get your shit packed and ready. I'll make the calls letting everyone know we're still on schedule for the tour and show tomorrow. You get ready to sell out stadiums and I promise you, I'll find out what happened to Courtney."

"Thanks, man. I don't know what I would do without you, Lorenzo."

"You'll never be without me so don't even put no energy in worrying about that. I'm about to go and make sure shit is straight for you, but I'll call and confirm everything."

"Cool. Philly here I come!" Phenomenon put on a brave front for Lorenzo masking the crying he was doing on the inside.

Lorenzo left Phenomenon's place feeling sick for his friend. He wanted answers to what happened to Courtney. Part of him wanted to believe Courtney started thinking things were moving too fast between her and Phenomenon and bailed on their relationship, but he knew that wasn't true. Courtney actually believed he was the best thing that ever happened to her and she wanted to make sure that her and Phenomenon walked down the aisle sooner rather than later. That only left one explanation for her sudden disappearance, which was foul play. Lorenzo was so deep in thought that he didn't even feel his phone vibrating. It wasn't until the person called back that Lorenzo realized he missed the initial call.

"Speak," Lorenzo answered.

"For a second I thought you were ignoring my calls," Ace said.

"Nah, I didn't hear my phone, but I hope you not calling to waste my time."

"I'll admit things are taking longer than usual, but these cases you got me working on are trickier than normal."

"Do you have some information for me or not?"

"I do have something."

"Then tell me what it is!" Lorenzo barked, becoming agitated.

"Erick Dolphin is a self-made man with a shit load of money. He makes a ton of investments..."

"Fuck all that shit," Lorenzo huffed cutting Ace off. "Just tell me the shit that I don't know. Like about his personal fuckin' life."

"He is a recovering addict who has done a lot of work at the Rockview Rehab facility."

"Why does that place sound so familiar?"

"Because it's the same rehab that Dior received treatment at."

"That's right. He must be the same Erick she was involved with."

"Yes, he is. They were living together. He is also the one responsible for getting her the role on *Baller Chicks*."

"It makes sense why he has such a hard on for me."

"What do you want me to do?"

"Get rid of him, but not just yet. I'll let you know when to make a move. What else you got?"

"Unfortunately, I still haven't been able to get much information about Carmen's daughter, but I'm going to have one of my people meet with the grandmother this week. She's been out of town, but one of her neighbors said she's suppose to be back this week."

"Alright, stay on top of that. Anything else?"

"Yes. There hasn't been any recent activity from Courtney, but after a lot of digging I was able to get a hold of her cell phone records. I know the last person Courtney called before she went missing."

"Who? Give me a name."

"She spoke to Lala."

"My Lala? The Lala I know?"

"Yes."

"Are you sure?"

"Positive. It was very brief, but it wasn't the

first time they spoke. Her phone records show that the two of them were speaking on a regular basis."

"I had no idea they were even in contact. I'll look into the Lala situation. You focus on finding out everything you can about Carmen's daughter. I'll be in touch when I'm ready for you to handle Erick Dolphin."

Lorenzo got into his car and kept thinking about Lala being the last person Courtney spoke to before she went missing. Something wasn't adding up. Lorenzo hadn't been in touch with Lala much since he told her he was going back to Dior, so she had no reason to mention to him that she had become cool with Courtney. But Lorenzo still wanted to speak with her because she might know something that could help them figure out what happened to Courtney. But the only person he wanted to speak to right now was Dior.

"Hello?"

"I'm finally able to get you on the phone."

"Lorenzo, it's so good to hear your voice. Where have you been? I've been waiting for you to call me."

"I called you a few times when I was supposed to come see you, but you never answered the phone. You know I'm not big on leaving messages, but I figured you would hit me back when you saw my missed calls. When you didn't, I thought maybe you decided to get back with that Erick dude I saw you kissing that night."

"I told you I was done with Erick. I wasn't able to call you back because I got in a car accident and while I was in the hospital I realized my phone was missing. I didn't have your phone number. When I finally got my phone back I was hoping and waiting for you to call but you never did."

"Baby, are you okay? I'm so sorry. I should've kept calling. Shit is so crazy for me right now. Phenomenon is freakin' out 'cause Courtney is missing and I'm figuring you straight over there in Hollywood land. Please forgive me."

"Of course I forgive you but Courtney is missing? Do you have any idea what happened to her?"

"I'm working on it. Please give me a couple of days and I'll be there with you."

"I hope so. I really need you. I want you to attend this award show with me. I was nominated for best new actress. I would love to have you by my side on the red carpet."

"Of course. I would feel honored to be by

your side."

"Thanks, babe. And Lorenzo, please know that you don't have to worry about Erick. It's over between him and me. I want my future to be with you."

"I want the same thing, but I think Erick is having a hard time accepting that."

"Why do you say that?"

"Because he is now heading up the record label Phenomenon is signed to and doing everything possible to fuck up his career. But I know he is really trying to fuck with me since Phenomenon is my artist."

"Oh gosh, I had no idea Erick would do something like that. I know you don't like anybody messing with your business. What are you going to do, Lorenzo?"

"What do you think I'ma do?"

"Please let me talk to him first."

"For what?"

"To see if I can get him to back down. He's done a lot for me, Lorenzo. I got clean because of him. If he ends of dead because of you then I'm going to feel responsible."

"You have nothing to feel responsible for. Erick is a grown ass man. If he wants to act like a tough guy, I'll show him what real tough guys do. He playin' wit' niggas lively hoods. Phenomenon don't deserve to be put in the middle of his make believe love triangle. You told him you was done wit' him. He needs to accept that shit and move the fuck on."

"You're right and you don't owe Erick anything, but I'm hoping you love me enough to this favor for me. Please," Dior begged.

"Fine, but if this shit ain't resolved with him in forty-eight hours, I'm moving forward with making Erick a non-issue."

"Thank you and Lorenzo... I love you."

"I love you, too. Lock my phone number in."

"I will." Dior laughed. "I'll talk to you soon."

Dior hung up with Lorenzo and her head was throbbing. She reached for one of her painkillers, but they were no longer giving her the fix she craved. She wanted something that would take the edge off. Dior remembered the coke that someone gave her at a party she attended a week ago. She had tossed it in her purse that day and now ran to her closet to retrieve it.

"There you are," Dior said taking the coke out of the small vial. "Maybe I need to toss this out," she said, debating with herself. Dior walked into the bathroom and lifted up the toilet. She continued debating with herself, but the white girl won the argument. Dior slammed down the toilet seat and headed to her living room. She sat on the edge of the couch and gently poured the white powder on the glass table in front of her. Dior rolled up a hundred dollar bill she had gotten from her wallet and began to snort. The moment it hit her bloodstream, the high Dior had desired was finally satisfied.

"Dior, what are you doing!" Tica shrieked in shock seeing her boss snorting coke.

"It's just a lil' coke. Hurry up and shut the door," Dior demanded as she continued getting her fix.

"I don't think you should be doing this," Tica said, thinking about the conversation she had with Courtney."

"I don't pay you to think, I pay you to do what I ask. And right now I'm asking you to go to that dealer friend of yours and score me some more coke," she said, reaching in her purse for some money.

Tica didn't argue with her boss. She simply took the money and did what she was asked. Dior on the other hand was relishing in her new high.

Chapter 18

No More Secrets

"When I called, I was so happy to hear you were in LA. I would much rather have this conversation in person than over the phone," Dior said when she got to Erick's mansion.

"I was happy when you called, but I can't say I was surprised. Have a seat outside," Erick said leading Dior through black framed French doors to a quiet terrace off the living room. It provided a peaceful retreat and stunning views.

"Before I tell you why I'm here, I have to say your home is beautiful. But I'm not surprised. The one we shared in New York was stunning, but I have to admit, I think I like this one better." Dior smiled looking around. She noticed a stucco archway with tall hedges surrounded by a hidden cloister.

Erick's Luxe Spanish-style mansion with sweeping coastal views was breathtaking. The tropical private estate sat behind a secure wall that was monitored by state of the art security. From the moment you drove up the brick paved driveway with fringed palms lining the entrance you were mesmerized. Marble floors covered the home's grand entryway and the wraparound staircase led to the second level. An infinity edge pool overlooked the warm waters of the bay where large yachts could be parked at each home's private dock.

"You know you're more than welcome to live here. I'm not in LA much and a lot of times this house is empty. I think you living here would be the perfect touch."

"Erick, that's sweet, but we both know that can't happen. Just like you purposely going after Lorenzo by trying to ruin Phenomenon's career can't happen."

"Is that what your boyfriend told you?"

"Is he lying?"

"Dior, it's strictly business."

"So it's a coincidence that you bought the same company that my boyfriend's artist is signed to. And you bought said company after I told you we were back together."

"Coincidences do happen. Like I said, it's business."

"I'll always appreciate everything you've done for me and as a courtesy I'm coming to you asking you to stop this vendetta you have against Lorenzo."

"Or what? You're boyfriend is going to retaliate? I'm not afraid of some thug like Lorenzo."

"And that's why I'm worried about you because you should be. I don't think you understand what type of man Lorenzo is."

"I know exactly what type of man he is and for the life of me I don't understand why you want to be with him."

"It's not for you to understand. I love him and he loves me. He has a good heart and would do anything for the people he cares about, but when it comes to his business... he's a different man."

"I can take care of myself."

"I don't want to see anything happen to you, Erick. I don't want this to be the way things end between us. I'm trying to be honest with you. Please, let this go. You're about to step into a world you don't want to be a part of. I'm not worth it." Dior felt herself getting a little sweaty and jittery.

"Are you using again?" Erick questioned, noticing Dior's demeanor and she had rubbed the tip of her nose more than a couple times since they sat down.

"Of course not."

"If you had a relapse, Dior, then you need to seek treatment immediately. If you don't, it's only going to get worse," Erick warned.

"I'm fine, but if you're really so concerned about me then you'll stop this pettiness with Lorenzo. He isn't to blame for our breakup. My heart always belonged to him and deep down you knew that. If you want to be mad at someone be mad at me ,but don't let it cost you your life."

"I'll do what you ask, Dior, but only because I don't like what this is doing to you. Whether you want to admit it or not, you're stressed out."

"I was in a car accident not too long ago."

"I know. Did you get the flowers I sent you?"

"Yes, I did. They were beautiful. I'm sorry I didn't call and thank you, but I lost all my phone contacts after the accident. I had to get your number from Tony."

"I understand and I feel terrible about that accident. But since we're being honest there's something you need to know."

"What is it?"

"Bianca had come to me saying she had a way of helping me get you back."

"Bianca! Why would she care one way or the other whether we got back together?"

"She said it would be beneficial to both of us."

"But how?"

"At the time I didn't know, but I decided I had no interest in working with Bianca and I would handle things my way. She called me a few times, but I never got back to her."

"Okay, so you didn't help Bianca out with her scheme. No harm no foul."

"The thing is Bianca took it way too far."

"I don't understand." Dior didn't know where Erick was going with this.

"Bianca is the one that was responsible for you car accident."

"That can't be right. Even she isn't that crazy."

"Yes, she is. When Tony told me about your accident it didn't sit well with me. I instantly thought about the last message Bianca left on my phone. She said since I wouldn't help she would handle the situation with you on her own. I brushed it off as Bianca having one of her typical temper tantrums. She's always been a drama queen, but after your accident that message she left meant a lot more. So I confronted her."

"What did she say?"

"She confessed. She wanted you off the show."

"I could've died in that accident!"

"Trust me, I read her the riot act. She claimed she only wanted to scare you, but the guys she hired took it too far."

"That evil bitch! I want her thrown under the jail cell."

"Dior wait!" Erick called, grabbing her arm. "If this came out it would ruin the show. Tony has worked so hard to make *Baller Chicks* a success."

"Does Tony know what Bianca did?"

"No, he doesn't. I agreed to keep Bianca's

secret if she promised to leave you alone. I told her if anything was to happen to you again that I would personally deal with her."

"That's not good enough. Bianca needs to pay for what she's done to me."

"Dior, I didn't have to tell you this."

"But you did."

"I told you because after you warned me about Lorenzo I felt I should come clean with you regarding Bianca. I also thought I could trust you with the information. The same way you asked me to step away from the Lorenzo situation and I agreed to, I'm asking you to let me deal with Bianca."

"This is completely different."

"Not really. We're both looking out for each other's best interest. If it comes out that Bianca was responsible for your accident then she will be arrested, the press will have a field day, and all the negative press will for sure make advertisers pull out and soon after the network will have no choice but to cancel *Baller Chicks*. Are you ready for the show to end?"

"No, I'm not. I love doing the show. I won't go to the police, but Bianca will be dealt with," Dior promised.

✦✦✦✦✦✦✦✦✦

Lorenzo had been trying to get in touch with Lala but had no luck. For the last couple of days he'd been meeting with Nico and Genesis trying to figure out who was behind the attack at the diner in Harlem. This was the first time he actually had a chance to stop by Lala's house. When he pulled up and knocked on the door nobody answered. He knew Lala kept a spare key under a small flowerpot in the entrance of the house so he used it to open the door.

"Lala... Tania!" he yelled out. "Is anybody home?" Nobody replied so Lorenzo began looking around. He wandered into the kitchen and noticed a desk in the corner. On top of a folder was a picture that caught his attention. It was a photo of a little girl and something about her seemed so familiar. Lorenzo was so transfixed on the photo that he didn't even hear Lala coming in.

"Lorenzo, what are you doing here?" she asked catching him off guard.

"I was looking for you. I've been calling you.

Why haven't you answered my calls?"

"I've been a little busy, you know."

"Where's Tania?"

"She's been staying with my mom. Like I said, I've been busy. What do you have in your hand?"

"A photo of a little girl. She's cute. Whose daughter is she?" Instead of answering, Lala put the grocery bag she had in her hand on top of the island.

"How did you get in here?"

"I remembered where you kept the spare key. After I kept calling and didn't hear from you I was concerned about you and Tania."

"Well, we're fine, but thanks for the concern. I should've called you back, but like I said, I've been busy. Is that all you wanted?"

"Actually, I also wanted to talk to you about Courtney."

"What about Courtney?"

"I'm sure you've heard by now that she's missing."

"I did hear about that. I figured she just needed to get away for a few days. She still hasn't showed up?"

"No, she hasn't."

"Phenomenon must be worried sick. But

I'm sure Courtney will show up soon. She does have a wedding to plan." Lala laughed nervously.

"I have one of my men trying to locate her and he told me that according to her cell phone records, you were the last person Courtney spoke to on the day she disappeared."

"Really? That's right I did talk to Courtney, but I had no idea that was the day she disappeared or that I was the last person she spoke to. Wow, that's pretty bizarre."

"I didn't know you and Courtney were friends."

"I wouldn't exactly describe us as friends. But that night we went to Phenomenon's place for dinner we became friendly."

"So, what did you all talk about the day she went missing? Maybe it can help us locate her."

"Nothing, really. It was a really brief conversation."

"Did she mention where she was going?"

"No, not that I can recall," Lala muttered becoming skittish.

"Are you nervous about something, Lala?"

"You're interrogating me like you're the police and I'm some sort of suspect. I really didn't mean to kill Courtney it was an accident." Those words slipped out of Lala's mouth as if she had no control over herself. But there was turning back now. The secret was out and there were more to come.

✦✦✦✦✦✦✦✦✦

"Where is Bianca?!" There was no camouflaging Dior's rage when she entered the dressing room on the set of *Baller Chicks*.

Neither Sherrie nor Destiny answered. They both sat in their chairs and continued getting their makeup done. Dior walked over and stood in front of both of them with fire in her eyes.

"I'm going to ask you trifling hoes one last time where Bianca is. If you don't answer, both of you will be eatin' that makeup." Dior had checked her Hollywood glamour girl persona at the front door and took it back to her roots, getting straight Philly hood chick on them.

"She's in the bathroom," they both blurted simultaneously.

Dior marched right to the bathroom door and didn't even bother to knock. When she opened it, Dior didn't even give her time to finish pulling up her panties. She dug her claws into Bianca's scalp almost ripping out her hair. "You dirty bitch!" Dior barked, flinging Bianca's body to the floor. She then dragged her out the bathroom into the middle of the dressing room where she began stomping Bianca like she stole her very last dollar.

"You're crazy! What is wrong with you!" Bianca wailed between blows as Dior continued to wreak havoc on her face and body.

Dior landed one last punch in Bianca's right jaw before putting the beating on pause. Blood was coming from Bianca's nose and mouth. She was too weak to try and fight back.

"I could've died because of you," Dior screamed, holding Bianca by the back of her neck. "You hired those men to run me off the road. You're the reason I was stuck in that hospital and bed-ridden! You better be happy you're not in jail or dead, you evil, sick, disgusting piece of shit!"

"Dior, let her go!" Tony yelled out as he and two security guards tried to pull Dior off of Bianca, but not before she landed one more solid punch to Bianca's eye.

"I bet yo' trifling ass won't fuck wit' me again!" Dior belted as they pulled her away.

"Dior, what has gotten into you? Why would you do that to Bianca?" Tony wanted to know.

"Because she is the reason I was run off the road. "

"What are you talking about?"

"Bianca wanted me off the show so she got the bright idea to hire some men to scare me by running me off the road. Erick told me everything."

"Bianca, is that true? Answer me!"

"I only wanted to scare her. I didn't think she would get hurt and end up in the hospital."

"Oh, Bianca, what have you done? Did you all have anything to do with it?" Tony turned his attention to Sherrie and Destiny.

"No! We swear. We were not involved," both ladies insisted.

"Dior, I'm sorry. I can't believe that Bianca would stoop that low."

"Don't apologize for her, Tony. This is all Bianca's doing. The only reason I'm not filing criminal charges is because I know that wouldn't be best for the show. But I will not work not one other day with Bianca. Either she goes or I go."

"Bianca, you're fired," Tony said without hesitation. "You have thirty minutes to clear out your dressing room and security will be escorting you out. Allison, get Carla on the phone. She'll be replacing Bianca."

"Thank you, Tony."

"No, thank you, Dior," he said kissing her on the cheek before leaving.

"I told you not to fuck with me, Bianca. I hope you ladies learned your lesson too," Dior said shooting Sherrie and Destiny death stares before exiting the room.

Chapter 19

Confessions

"Bitch, you gon' be shittin' on everybody to-morrow night when you hit that red carpet." Brittani gasped when Dior tried on her dress. Dior looked like a tall glass of champagne filled with diamonds in the silver Steven Khalil cutout gown that was covered in crystals. The hem fell below her ankle, flowing over her nudist sandals.

"This dress is fuckin' hot, right." Dior twirled around in front of the floor length mirror admiring every detail of the designer gown.

"Hot isn't even the right word to describe what you looking like. Wait 'til Lorenzo see you in this." Brittani smiled.

"I know. I'm so glad he's going to be here with me tomorrow to walk the red carpet. I need my man," Dior said, pouring herself another glass of Moscato. "Do you want some more?" Dior held out the bottle.

"No, I'm straight. Girl, it's only two in the afternoon. If I drink one more glass I might fall asleep." Brittani laughed.

"I know what you mean, but just one of these little pills will keep me wide awake." Dior giggled, popping the white pill in her mouth and dousing it down with wine.

"I thought you said you were done with painkillers, Dior?" Brittani asked turning serious.

"I have a prescription for these. I'm working crazy hours. I'm still in a little pain from the accident. They're harmless."

"So it's just pills, nothing else... like coke for instance?"

"I told you I was done with that," Dior lied. The only thing white I'm taking are these pills. I've left coke alone a long time ago."

"I wish you would leave all narcotics alone, but I rather you pop a pill every once in awhile than snort coke. You've come so far, Dior. I don't want you to slip back into that life."

"I hear you, Brittani, and I'm not. I'm good," Dior reassured her as she continued staring at her reflection in the mirror. "I'm a star now. I have everything under control."

❀❀❀❀❀❀❀❀❀❀

Lorenzo stood looking at Lala for a moment thinking that he misunderstood what she said. He couldn't even fathom that he heard her correctly.

"I did it for us, Lorenzo."

"You did what for us?" Lorenzo's tone was calm, but his expression couldn't hide his disbelief at what Lala was confessing to him.

"Killing Courtney and Carmen. Courtney just couldn't mind her business and threatened to go to you about her absurd suspicions. I wasn't going to let that happen. My plan was coming together and she was going to ruin everything. Then Carmen was supposed to kill

Dior, but she fucked it all up and killed the wrong person," Lala said shaking her head. "I had no choice but to get rid of her. Carmen was in love with you too and she wanted to take you from me. I couldn't let that happen."

"Carmen was supposed to kill Dior and it was you that killed Carmen." Lorenzo stated, taking a seat trying to wrap his mind around what Lala was saying.

"I know this is coming as a shock to you, but if we're going to move forward as a family I had to be honest with you."

"You still haven't answered my question. That photo of the little girl I found on the desk, who is she?"

"Carmen's daughter."

"Why would you have a picture of Carmen's daughter and how did you get it?"

"Carmen didn't want you to know about her so she kept her away. I was only finishing what she started."

"Why wouldn't Carmen want me to know about her daughter?"

"After I killed Carmen, the little girl came running down the stairs. As soon as I saw her face I knew she was yours. When you looked at the photo I bet you thought the same thing."

"You're lying. I don't know what type of game you playin', Lala, but this is bullshit. Carmen wouldn't have my child and keep that from me." Lorenzo was in denial. He didn't want to believe that Lala was the psycho she was revealing herself to be or that Carmen would've kept his child from him.

"I'm telling the truth. Carmen lied to you for all those years. She wasn't worthy of you and neither is Dior. I was hoping you would forget about her. Let her go off to Hollywood and be the industry slut that she is. But no, you just couldn't let go. You always leave me no choice but to clean up your messes."

"Lala, what are you talkin' about... what messes? What else have you done?" Lorenzo was spilling over in anger, but he was trying to keep it in check. He now knew for a fact that Lala was unstable and he wanted to get all the information out of her he could before she completely lost it.

"Like I said, I did everything for us so we can be a family. Me, you and Tania."

"What about my daughter? Shouldn't she be a part of our family too?"

"I couldn't let that happen, Lorenzo. She would've constantly been a reminder of what you shared with Carmen. It would've ruined our family. We needed a fresh start without anyone from your past."

"Where's my daughter, Lala?"

"She's with her mother now."

"What do you mean she's with her mother now?"

"Once I had proof she was your daughter I knew eventually you would find out and want to be a part of her life. I couldn't let that happen so I had her sent to kiddy heaven. She's at peace now."

"You sick bitch. You killed my daughter," Lorenzo stated as if in a daze. "I never even had a chance to lay eyes on her," Lorenzo said as his voice cracked.

"You think I'm sick. You made me this way. You made me fall in love with you. Now I'm supposed to let you go live some happily ever after with a Hollywood home wrecking slut like Dior. You belong with me! You took Darell away from me and left my daughter without a father. You owe me."

"What are you talking about... Alexus killed Darell."

"You fuckin' liar! You lie with such ease like it's second nature to you. Alexus didn't kill

Darell, you did. I heard you that night talking to Phenomenon. All this time you made me believe it was Alexus, but it was you. You took away the only man that ever truly loved me and you left Tania without her father. You know how different my life would be right now if Darell was still alive."

"Lala, I'm sorry. Killing Darell was a mistake and I have to learn to live with the guilt for the rest of my life."

"No worries. That's the past and we should leave it there. We've both made mistakes, but I forgive you and I know in time you'll forgive me too. The two of us and Tania can now be a family and have our happy ending."

"Lala, there is no us. You killed Carmen for nothing. You took my daughter from me for nothing. I'm still leaving and I'm still going to build my life with Dior so you did all this for nothing. Nothing! Do you understand that?" Lorenzo belted, storming towards Lala.

"It wasn't for nothing. If you won't give me my happily ever after then you won't have one either," Lala threatened, reaching into her purse and pulling out her gun.

✿✿✿✿✿✿✿✿✿✿

"Why aren't you answering your phone," Dior huffed, as she tried calling Lorenzo for the third time. Dior was on Pacific Coast Highway in Malibu on her way to meet with Tony and Max to discuss a new project they wanted her to star in. Although she was excited to know the details, her mind was more focused on Lorenzo and what time his flight would be getting in tomorrow.

"Baby, please answer your phone. I need to hear your voice and know that you'll be here for me tomorrow night," Dior said out loud as she continued calling Lorenzo's cell. Dior had walked many red carpets, especially since the show *Baller Chicks* became a huge success, but tomorrow night was different. Dior had been nominated for a best new actress award in a series. She needed her man by her side. As her nerves got the best of her, Dior reached in her purse and pulled out a vile of cocaine that was disguised as lipstick. She took a couple of quick snorts before pulling off on her exit.

Lala brandishing her weapon stopped Lorenzo dead in his tracks. His fury made him forget for a second that he was dealing with a nutcase. He shifted from his calm demeanor and showed his true colors. Now Lala had a 9mm pointed directly at him and with him being unarmed, Lorenzo had to use his next best weapon, which was his mouthpiece.

"Lala, what are you doing? We're better than this. We've been through too much together for it to end like this," Lorenzo said, trying to reason with a crazy person.

"What are you saying, Lorenzo, that you forgive me for killing Carmen and having your daughter murdered?"

"Yes, I do. I understand why you did it. You want us to be a family. The family I took away from you. I never forgave myself for killing Darell and you're right, I need to step up and be there for you and Tania."

"I'm glad you're seeing things my way."

"I am, Lala."

"So you're not leaving me for Dior."

"No. It's over for Dior and me. As soon as you put down the gun I'm going to call Dior and let her know it's over between us and that you're the person I'm going to spend the rest of my life with," Lorenzo assured her.

"No need to call her. I've taken care of Dior. She won't be a problem for us ever again. I just wanted to see if you were willing to choose me over her."

"Lala, what do you mean you've taken care of Dior?" Lorenzo inquired.

"Why do you care?"

"Curious that's all."

"It doesn't matter. You've chosen me!" Lala screamed out.

"Chill. I thought we were being honest with each other. If we want to move forward there shouldn't be any secrets between us right?"

"Stop questioning me about Dior. You chose me, unless you're lying to me. Are you lying, Lorenzo? Answer me!" Lala continued scream-ing, becoming louder and more upset. It was obvious that Lorenzo wasn't going to be able to talk her down. Lala's hands were trembling and if he was going to make a move, it needed to happen soon before this turned into some sort of murder-suicide.

"I'm sorry, Lala. You're right, Dior is the past, there is no need to discuss her," Lorenzo said trying to calm the situation, but Lala had already gone over the edge.

"Shut up! Just shut up, Lorenzo! You're lying to me. But you'll never have your precious Dior. Never! You'll never get your happy ending," As Lala continued with her over the top tantrum, Lorenzo used the opportunity to lunge forward and wrangle the gun out of Lala's hand. But you can never underestimate the vigor of a crazy person. Lala had seemed to develop supernatural strength as she tussled with Lorenzo to keep a hold of the gun before pulling the trigger. The gunshot sounded like a muffled explosion, shocking both Lorenzo and Lala.

❈❈❈❈❈❈❈❈❈❈

"Dior, you looking stunning as usual." Max smiled. He greeted her with a hug when Dior sat down. Max and Tony were outside by the pool having lunch when Dior arrived. Max had already informed his maid that Dior would be joining them so she quickly brought out her food once Dior was seated.

"You do look amazing. This LA weather has done wonders for your skin and hair," Tony chimed in.

"Flattery will get the two of you everything." Dior giggled. There was no denying she did look stunning in a mid-thigh white tuxedo dress that had four oversized black buttons. The Jimmy Choo Amika pumps are what really set the look off. The black lace on the sides with leather toe cap and four inch heels took the simple yet sexy dress to the next level.

"As you both know, I don't like to waste time on small talk so let's get right to it," Max stated, taking a sip of his champagne. Dior was thrilled there was a glass already filled for her because for whatever reason when Dior snorted coke she loved to chase it with the bubbly or vise versa.

"By all means do tell what this new project is about," Dior said, gulping down her champagne and waving her finger for a refill.

"We're all aware how successful *Baller Chicks* has been and Dior you deserve most of the credit for that."

"Yes, she does," Tony said, nodding his head.

"And the way you handled the Bianca situation was admirable. It showed what a team player you are, not wanting the show to get such bad publicity."

"Thank you so much, both of you." Dior smiled, very humbled by them crediting her for the success of the show. She had no further comment when it came to Bianca's evil ass. The unmerciful whooping she gave her did all the talking for her.

"Don't thank us, we thank you and to show our appreciation we want to offer you a spin off."

"Excuse me?" Dior questioned, almost spitting out her champagne due to her shock.

"You heard me," Max said, repeating himself. "We want to offer you a spin off, your own show. I believe you can carry your own show and so does Tony." Tony shook his head agreeing with Max. "So what do you say?"

"I say hell yeah!"

"Wonderful!" both Max and Tony said simultaneously. "Let's toast to the next level of your career, Dior."

"Yes, to the next level," Dior beamed. She was astonished that all her dreams and beyond were coming true.

Chapter 20

Déjà vu

"I love you, Lorenzo... forever," Lala mumbled before falling to the floor. When her body hit the hardwood, Lorenzo looked down as the blood spilled from her abdomen. A single shot had ripped through her stomach killing Lala almost instantly. When they were struggling for the gun, Lorenzo wanted to live, but he also didn't want Lala to die, mainly for Tania's sake. He loved Tania and never would he want her to lose her mother, not like this. At the same time, a part of Lorenzo thought this might be for the best. He didn't see how any good could come out of Tania growing up having to visit her mother behind bars. Lorenzo had so many incomplete thoughts running through his brain. The only thing he knew for certain was that he had to get to Dior.

✿✿✿✿✿✿✿✿✿

"Have you spoken to Lorenzo yet?" Tica questioned as she was organizing Dior's clothes and accessories for tomorrow's event.

"No, not yet. I'm starting to think something might be wrong. It's not like him to not answer my calls or text messages. I hope everything is okay," Dior said leaning over the nightstand in her bedroom and sniffing a line.

"Do you need me to get you some more?" Tica asked, as she lined up three different pair of shoes for Dior to choose from.

"No, I still have plenty left from the last batch you got for me," Dior answered, about to take another sniff before hearing her cell ring.

"Finally!" she barked, answering her phone. "Where have you been?" Dior yelled.

"Babe, I'm so sorry. Some crazy shit went down earlier today and I'm just clearing this shit up," Lorenzo explained.

"What crazy shit went down?"

"I'll explain when I get there. All I want to know is that you're okay?"

"I'm fine. I was worried about you," Dior sighed.

"Baby, I'm sorry. But until I get there I really need for you to be careful."

"Lorenzo, you're scaring me. What's going on?" Lorenzo's warning had Dior puzzled.

"Don't be scared just careful. But my flight is leaving in a couple of hours so I'll be to you soon."

"I'm so glad you're coming. I was afraid you wouldn't be here and I need you."

"Dior, I wouldn't miss this. I'll be there for you. I promise."

"What time do I need to pick you up from the airport?" Dior questioned, excited that she would finally get to see Lorenzo.

"I got all that handled. Just do one favor for me," Lorenzo said.

"Sure what is it?"

"Stay in until I get there. Don't go out. Please."

"Okay, baby. Just get here. I miss you."

"Miss you, too. See you soon."

"Is everything okay?" Tica asked when Dior ended her call.

"Everything is perfect! My baby will be here tonight so all is great!" Dior smiled, kicking her legs up in the air as she lay on the bed.

"Oh good. You had me worried for a second," Tica commented, hanging up Dior's dress.

"You can go 'head and go, Tica. You can finish this up tomorrow."

"Are you sure? Tomorrow is the big day. I want everything to be to your liking."

"I know, but tonight is also my big day. My man is coming home to me and I want to make sure I have everything ready for him, which is me. So you can go. I need to pamper myself."

"Got you. I'll wait for your call before coming over. Of course ring me if you need me."

"Will do and thanks, Tica. I'll see you tomorrow," Dior said heading towards the shower as Tica let herself out. When Dior got in the shower and let the hot water saturate her body, she closed her eyes yearning for the moment she would be with Lorenzo again.

✿✿✿✿✿✿✿✿✿✿

Lorenzo slowly turned the key to open the front door. He had tried calling Dior when the plane landed but got no answer. His flight had been delayed and figured Dior had fallen asleep. When he got inside of her condo, he headed towards the bedroom and as he expected Dior was sleep. She looked so peaceful lying there in a sheer baby blue lingerie. The silk sheets were draping right beneath her hips exposing the curves of her body. Lorenzo wanted to slide inside of Dior right then, but after the long flight, a shower was calling his name.

Once Lorenzo got out the shower, he headed straight to a sleeping Dior and gently placed his lips on hers. It wasn't until Lorenzo began sprinkling her neck with kisses that Dior began waking up.

"Baby, you made it," Dior said softly opening her eyes.

"Yes. Nothing was gonna keep me away from you," Lorenzo replied, taking her hardened nipple in his mouth. The feel of his wet

187

tongue circling her breast made Dior's body shiver. Lorenzo took his time caressing, stroking, and simply touching every inch of her body, not missing a single spot.

When he entered inside of her, Lorenzo moved with ease wanting to savor how warm and wet Dior's walls felt around his rock hard dick.

"Ooh," Dior purred as her pleasure elevated. She could've relished in Lorenzo's thrusting all night and the louder she moaned the more intense Lorenzo's strokes became. The two of them became lost in each other's embrace and seemed to make love forever.

"Good morning, beautiful," Lorenzo said dangling a bag in Dior's face.

"What's this?" she smiled, sitting up in bed.

"There was nothing in your refrigerator, so I went to the bakery across the street and got some warm croissants and fresh fruit," Lorenzo said opening the bag.

"How sweet are you. All I need is a mimosa to wash this down."

"Sorry, babe, but they weren't selling that. All I have is some OJ."

"That's all I need. I keep champagne stocked." Dior laughed, giving Lorenzo a kiss before hopping out the bed and going in the kitchen. "Would you like a glass, too?" she called out.

"No, I'm straight," he yelled back. Lorenzo then grabbed the bag and went to the kitchen where Dior was. "I knew I missed you, but I didn't know just how much until last night," Lorenzo said, walking up behind Dior in the kitchen and wrapping his arms around her waist.

"Well, I knew how much I missed you. If I didn't hear from you soon, I was going to get on a plane and drag you out of New York."

"Is that right?"

"Yep!" Dior said, sipping the mimosa she just finished making. "I don't ever want us to be apart this long again. I don't feel complete without you."

"I know what you mean. These last couple of days so much crazy shit has gone down and it made me put a lot of things in perspective."

"Things like what? Does it have anything to do with what you were talking about last night on the phone?" she questioned, turning around to face Lorenzo.

"Babe, there's a couple of things I want to tell you, but I don't want you freaking out."

"Okay, tell me," Dior said feeling anxious.

"Let's go sit down." Lorenzo took Dior's hand and led her over to the couch. "I was still having some dealings with Lala."

"Lala, the woman who taunted me when the police came to arrest you... that Lala?"

"Yes." Lorenzo didn't want to admit that to Dior, but under the circumstances he didn't feel like he had a choice. "During the time I thought you were dead we reconnected. She came through for me on the court shit. Wouldn't testify against me and she was one of the main reasons I got out. I felt that I owed her for a lot of reasons."

"What about when we got back together?" Dior questioned almost afraid to hear the answer.

"In the beginning, I dabbled a little. After that Erick situation I slipped. But when I knew without a doubt that we were in it for the long haul, I let Lala know that my heart was with you. I put that on everything."

"Why are you telling me all of this now?" Dior wanted to know as she tried her hardest to keep her composure.

"Lala is dead. But yesterday before she died I found out a few things. This girl Carmen who I used to do business with and fuck with had been working with Lala. She was the one who tried to kill you at the Celebrity Bash party."

"What!" Dior exclaimed. Standing up in disbelief.

"I know, I was stunned too. But it gets crazier."

"I don't see how it could," Dior said, shaking her head. She wasn't prepared for all this news Lorenzo was dropping on her.

"It does. After Carmen killed the wrong girl, Lala decided to kill Carmen. Not only that. I found out that Carmen had a baby by me that I knew nothing about for all these years."

"Wait a minute... you have a child?"

"I had a daughter. She was six years old."

"What do you mean had?"

"It's hard for me to even say this." Lorenzo put his head down for a minute, getting choked up thinking about it. "Lala had my daughter killed."

Dior's eyes widened as she digested what she had just learned. "Lorenzo, I'm so sorry."

"I also think she might've been plotting on how to hurt you."

"Besides my accident which I told you Bianca was responsible for nothing strange has happened to me."

"I know, but my gut is telling me we shouldn't put our guards down."

"You think I'm still in danger?"

"I can't say for sure. That's why I wanted you to lay low until I got here. I wasn't sure if Lala still had someone out there trying to hurt you."

"Clearly Lala's crazy, but she's dead now. Don't you think that's all behind us?" Dior hoped.

"I want to believe that, but it was something Lala said before she died that I can't shake," Lorenzo said, biting down on his bottom lip.

"What did Lala say?" Dior asked.

"She said we would never have our happy ending."

"I'm sure she was just talking crazy to get under your skin. There's nothing she can do now. We're here together and she's dead. You didn't tell me how she died though."

"We struggled with the gun and it went off killing her."

"I need another drink," Dior scoffed.

"I know I hit you with a lot, but are you okay?" Lorenzo questioned knowing in his heart that Dior wasn't.

"I'm fine," Dior lied. Although she was putting on a strong front, inside Dior was crushed. She was flooded with memories of when Lala told her that Lorenzo never really loved her that he was only with her because he felt sorry for her.

"I have to run out and get fitted for the suit I'm wearing tonight. I shouldn't be gone that long. Will you be okay?" Lorenzo took Dior's hand. "You're trembling," he said, full of concern. "Why don't you come with me?"

"I can't. I need to get some things done before the awards show tonight. Go get fitted for your suit. I'll be fine."

"Are you sure, Dior?"

"Yes."

"I love you."

"I love you more."

"Never more," Lorenzo said, kissing Dior on the lips before leaving.

Dior didn't even wait five seconds before going to her dresser drawer to retrieve her stash. She was desperately craving to do a line or two if only to take the edge off.

"What the fuck!" Dior screamed out loud when she opened the drawer and looked inside a jewelry box she kept her coke and pills in to find nothing there. "I know I put it here," she said talking to herself out loud. Dior began rummaging through all her drawers, closets, and any place else in search of her stash. She felt like her head was going to explode. Dior ran back into her bedroom to get her cell phone.

"Hey! You ready for me to come over?" Tica said when she answered Dior's call.

"Have you seen my stash?" Dior questioned getting straight to the point.

"No. I thought you were out, but you told me yesterday that you still had some left from before."

"I can't find it anywhere. I could've sworn I left it in my jewelry box." Dior's mind switched to Lorenzo for a second. *Could Lorenzo have found my stash and gotten rid of it? Oh gosh! I can't think about that right now*, Dior thought to herself.

"Dior, are you there?"

"Yes, I'm here. Listen, I need you to do something for me."

"Sure what is it?"

"On your way over here stop and get me some white girl." Dior directed Tica.

"No problem."

"I need it now. So hurry up before Lorenzo gets back," Dior stated and ended the call.

Dior took a shower, ate her croissants, made a few phone calls trying to keep herself busy while she waited for Tica. Dior was about to pour herself another drink when she heard the front door opening. Her fingers were crossed hoping it was Tica and not Lorenzo since both had a key. She rushed to the door.

"Sorry it took me so long, but the guy got held up with another client. I was able..." before Tica could even finish, Dior had snatched the bag out of her hand and went into her bedroom and closed the door. After taking the coke out, Dior spread a few lines on the bathroom counter. She knew Lorenzo would be back soon and wanted to get her fix before he popped back up. The white girl was calling Dior's name and she responded by filling her nostrils with the powder.

"Hello," Lorenzo said to Tica when he entered the condo.

"Hi! You must be Lorenzo," Tica said nervously.

"I am and you are?"

"Tica, Dior's assistant."

"Oh, where is Dior?"

"I think she's taking a shower."

"Okay," Lorenzo said heading towards the bedroom."

"She closed the door and said she didn't want to be disturbed," Tica yelled out, trying to stop Lorenzo from going inside.

"That doesn't apply to me," he stated, brushing Tica's comment off. "Babe, I'm back, Lorenzo called out when he got in the bedroom. Dior wasn't in there so he looked at the bathroom door, which was closed. When Lorenzo tried to open it, the door was locked. He didn't hear the shower so he knocked. "Dior, open the door!" he shouted when he didn't get an answer. Lorenzo began banging and pounding on the door with no response.

"Is everything okay in here!" Tica asked in a frantic voice.

"No! Dior ain't opening the fuckin' door," Lorenzo belted.

"I told you she was in the shower," Tica stuttered.

"She ain't in no fuckin' shower! What the hell is going on!" Lorenzo demanded as he continued pounding his fist on the door.

"I think I better go," Tica mumbled, turning around to make her exit.

Lorenzo quickly reached out his hand and grabbed Tica's arm. "Where the fuck do you think you're going? You ain't going nowhere until I open this bathroom door."

Tica swallowed hard seeing the rage in Lorenzo's eyes. Lorenzo then lifted up his leg and began trying to kick open the door. After the third kick, Lorenzo busted open the door.

"Oh gosh! Is she dead!" Tica wailed, covering her mouth with her hands.

Lorenzo rushed over to Dior's limp body, sprawled on the bathroom floor. "Baby, no! No! No! No!" Lorenzo quickly noticed the white powder on the bathroom sink and on Dior's nose. "Call 911 and get some fuckin' help!" Lorenzo hollered to Tica.

"Okay! I'll call right now!"

"Dior, baby, please. You can't leave me...not like this." Lorenzo began administrating CPR trying to revive Dior, but she seemed gone."

"They're on the way," Tica ran back in the bedroom and said breathing heavily.

"Where did she get these drugs from?" Lorenzo asked Tica.

"I don't now."

"Don't fuckin' lie to me or I'll break your neck. Where did Dior get these drugs? Answer me!" Lorenzo barked. Instead of answering, Tica took off running and Lorenzo was right on her ass.

"Get away from me!" Tica cried out, but before she knew it, Lorenzo had her pinned up against the wall.

"Where did Dior get those fuckin' drugs!"

"I gave them to her, but she asked me to," Tica whimpered.

"What the fuck did you give her because some cocaine wouldn't have her dead on the bathroom floor. Answer me!" Lorenzo shouted, slamming Tica against the wall.

"I got a lot of perks working for Dior, but the salary sucked. I needed the money. I told her Dior was back using and she gave me twenty-five thousand dollars to give her some bad drugs. I didn't think she would die. It was just so you could find out she was back using," Tica sobbed. "She hoped once she found out, you would be done with Dior for good."

"Who paid you... was it Lala?"

"Yes," Tica conceded in a low tone.

Lorenzo was about to break Tica's neck when he heard the police banging on the door. Tica knew she had been knocking on death's door and was grateful the police showed up when they did.

"She's in the bathroom," Lorenzo pointed towards the bedroom when he let the police and paramedics in. His voice was somber when he spoke to them as if all life had been drained from his body. "I did everything I could, but I couldn't save her," Lorenzo told the cops with tears in his eyes.

"Move out the way, sir," one of the paramedics said as they rushed to the bathroom.

Lorenzo sat on the couch answering the police's questions as best as possible, on the verge of crumbling. All he could think was that Lala had won. He would never get his happily ever after with Dior.

Epilogue

Now & Forever

Six Months Later...

Dior sat on the bench of the outside garden at the Rockview Rehabilitation Center. It was like déjà vu all over again. Never did Dior believe she would find herself back there, sitting on the exact bench that she shared so many intimate details with her drug counselor. But here she was, fighting to hold on to her sobriety. But this time Dior didn't want to just win the battle, she planned on winning the war.

"Can I join you?" a familiar voice startled Dior out of her deep thoughts.

"Lorenzo, what are you doing here?"

"Why do you think I'm here... I'm here for you," he said, sitting next to Dior on the bench. She put her head down as if in shame. "Why are you looking down? I want to see those big beautiful eyes," Lorenzo said, lifting Dior's chin.

"Look at me, there's nothing beautiful about me," Dior said, trying to turn her head.

"That's where you're wrong. You're more beautiful now than you've ever been."

"You don't have to say that, especially since I know you don't mean it."

"That's where you're wrong, Dior." They both remained silent for a few minutes looking out at the lush acres filled with gardens, lakes, and a mollifying yet stunning waterfall. It was supported by huge rocks which split into two Mediterranean style ponds with a curved stream running through it. The landscape gave a mountain feel that seemed more like a romantic getaway then a drug addict's last chance at survival.

"I've been doing a lot of thinking since you've been here."

"Me too." Dior smiled. "That's all I've been doing."

"I was so angry at myself," Lorenzo admitted.

"Why were you angry at yourself? If anything you should've been angry with me."

"Because I felt that for the second time I had let you down. First, when I went to jail and you got caught up with Sway again, and then I let all those Hollywood vultures get in your ear and I didn't protect you from Lala."

"That wasn't your fault and neither was my overdose. Besides the fact that I shouldn't have been doing drugs in the first place, the only other person to blame is Lala. How were you supposed to know she was insane? You can't protect me from crazy especially if you have no idea what you're dealing with. I still can't believe that she paid my assistant... I mean my former assistant to give me bad drugs. That woman was sick. I almost died. I'm so happy Tica is behind bars where she belongs."

"All that is true, but I should've been there for you, Dior. You told me in every way you could that you needed me, but I wasn't listening. You seemed to be living your dreams and I took that shit for granted that you had everything together. I fell for the hype. It wasn't until I found you in the bathroom and I thought you were dead did I realize you had been crying out for my help. Baby, I'm so sorry I let you down," Lorenzo said as his eyes watered up.

"You have nothing to apologize for. I'm an addict, Lorenzo. It took me all these years and me almost dying for the second time to get it, but now I do. I will always be an addict. That's something I have to accept. It will forever be a daily battle for me."

"Can we fight that battle together?" Lorenzo asked.

"After everything I've put you through, you still want to be with me?" Dior questioned, totally stunned.

"Not only do I want to be with you, I want you to be my wife." Lorenzo then reached in his pocket and pulled out a small black velvet box and opened it while getting on bended knee. "Will you marry me, Dior?"

"I'm so blinded by the size of that diamond, I can't even think!" Dior laughed nervously.

"That's not an answer." Lorenzo smiled, still on bended knee.

"For so long I wanted fame and stardom. I thought that would give me everything my heart desired. Once I achieved all that, I realized how wrong I was. I don't want or need the stardom. I choose love... I choose you. Yes, yes, Lorenzo, I'll marry you," Dior beamed.

"Baby, thank you for choosing me, but please know you can have both, if that's what you want. If the fame and having a career as an actress is what you want, I have your back. I don't want you to think that it's either, or. I don't ever want you to feel that you had to give up fulfilling your dreams for me."

"Thank you for saying that. Knowing I have your support means the world to me. Honestly, I'm not sure what I want to do about my career. Max and Tony still want me to do my own spin off show, but I don't know if that's what I want anymore. My sobriety is the most important thing. I have to take it one day at a time. The only thing I am one hundred percent sure about is that I want to be your wife." Dior smiled.

Lorenzo slid the massive rock on Dior's finger before they embraced. They then locked lips, but it was much deeper than their normal passionate kisses. Dior's near death experience made them bond and connect on a whole other level. They held each other as if never wanting to let go.

"Now that we're getting married, it's forever," Dior said sweetly.

"That's the plan when I put this ring on your finger. It's 'til death do us part. You will be my first, my last, and only wife. We will get through this recovery together and it will make our bond unbreakable. That I promise you," Lorenzo stated confidently.

"I believe you. You know what I'm looking forward to?"

"What?" Lorenzo asked, pulling Dior even closer.

"I'm ready for us to have a little Lorenzo or Dior running around."

"Are you serious?"

"Yes. I'm ready to be a wife and mother to your child. I've learned so much about myself and because of you, I know that we can get through anything."

"Yes, we can. I love you, Dior."

"I love you, too, Lorenzo."

The End

Chapter 1

I Got A Story To Tell

I came into this world wanting one thing... love. I couldn't get that love from my mother so I stole it from the streets. Eventually, I did get the love, respect, and money I craved, but it came at a very high price. As I stand here today, I can't help but ask myself, was it worth it? But before I can answer that question and move forward, I have to go back to what brought me here.

"Nico, get yo' ass in this house," my mother yelled out the window.

"I'm coming!" I yelled back for the third time, running with the ball in my hands, knowing I was lying again. We were playing the hood version of football and my team was winning so I didn't want to stop. See, the older boys in the neighborhood thought they could kick our ass 'cause we were young.

My boy Lance and I were only 10, but we were both tall for our age, fast, and already had a lil' muscle tone. My best friend, Ritchie, and the other boys on our team were either below average or average at best. But with Lance and my skills and the other boys just following our lead, we would constantly beat the older boys. It would drive them crazy and I loved it.

"Touch down!" I hollered and started doing my signature two-step dance move before throwing the ball down. "Peace out motherfuckers!" I grinned, before running towards my apartment.

"We see you tomorrow!" I heard Ritchie and the other boys yell back.

"Boy, you see what time it is?" my mother popped as soon as I closed the door. "You know you ain't supposed to be outside when it get this dark."

"Sorry. I was playing football and didn't realize it was so late."

"Well go in there and get yo'self cleaned up. Yo' daddy will be over here in a little bit," my mom said, fixing her hair in the mirror.

"Now it makes sense," I mumbled.

"What you say, boy?" my mother said, shooting me one of her evil looks.

"I just said I was hungry," I lied.

"I'm sure yo' daddy will take us out to eat when he gets here. So hurry up! I want you to be clean, dressed, and ready when he walk through that door."

I was wondering why my mom was so concerned about me coming in the house. Normally, I could come home at any time of the night and she wouldn't notice or care. She would assume I was at Ritchie's house or another kid in the building and it almost felt like she preferred I stayed there. The only time she wanted me around was if my father was coming over to visit. She would always put on this big show as if she was the Mother Of The Year. I would play along because part of me was always hoping that maybe one day her pretending would rub off and become a reality.

After taking a bath, I decided to put on the New York Knicks jersey my dad had gotten me. I smiled looking at myself in the mirror. I was the spitting image of my father and that made me feel proud.

"Where my lil' man Nico at!" I heard my father call out.

"What up, Dad!" I said, running up to him. He wrapped his strong arms around me giving me a hug like only he could.

"I just saw you a couple days ago and you already grew a few inches. Damn, you a handsome kid, if I say so myself." My dad smiled proudly.

"You only saying that 'cause he look just like you." My mother laughed.

"But of course. Nico know where he get them good looks from, don't you boy," my dad teased, putting his huge hand on top of my head and playfully shaking it. "You ready to go?"

"Yes, sir. Where we going?"

"I got us tickets to go see the Yankees play."

"No way!"

"Do I ever lie to you?"

"Nope, you sure don't, Daddy."

"And I never will. Now let's get outta here."

"Nico said he was hungry. I thought the three of us would go get something to eat," my mother said, folding her arms.

"Maybe next time, Shaniece. Tonight it's just me and my son," my dad said, taking my hand. When I turned to tell my mother bye, she was rolling her eyes.

"What you mean maybe next time? Don't you see me dressed? You think I got all jazzed up to sit in this apartment?"

"Here, go out and have a good time wit' your girlfriends. Nico can stay with me for the night," my dad said, giving my mother a bunch of money. She balled it up in her fist tightly, but I could tell she was steaming mad.

"Fine, you keep him, but you still owe me dinner," she snapped, putting her other hand on her hip.

"See you tomorrow, Mom," I said about to go give her a hug goodbye, but she walked away. I took my dad's hand and we left.

My dad had recently bought a new gold, two door Mercedes Benz sedan and this was the first time I was going for a ride in it. Last week when he stopped by so I could see it, everybody went crazy on the block. My dad was the man and when I grew up I wanted to be just like him. After we got in the car and settled in my dad turned on the radio. But before I could start jamming to the beat, he turned the music down and looked at me.

"Nico, I want you to know something," he said with a stone face. My dad was always smiling and joking so it was weird seeing him so serious.

"What is it, Dad?"

"You're my son, my only child and I love you no matter what."

"I know and I love you, too."

"You might not be seeing me around at your mother's place that much anymore, but I want you to come stay at my house on the weekends. Is that okay with you?"

"Yes! I just wanna spend time with you. I don't care where."

"That's my boy. Now let's go see these Yankees." My dad smiled and drove off.

Although I was young, I knew exactly what was going on. Ever since I could remember my mother and father were on and off. They never lived together and half the time they were arguing and the other half they were in the bedroom with the door locked. I guess they were about to be off again. My dad had never told me he wasn't going to be coming around, so something had changed, I just didn't know what.

A KING PRODUCTION

All I See Is The Money...

Female Hustler

A Novel

JOY DEJA KING

Chapter One

Butterfly Effect

The butterfly effect suggests that small, unnoticeable causes may contribute to huge, unpredictable effects, which is also known as the chaos theory. This analysis may be viewed one way in scientific terms, but if you flip the coin to the other side, the same rules apply when it comes to the journey of life and Angel Riviera was living proof of that.

Angel's life and the lives of others would forever be altered based on one decision, that at the time it was made, Angel's mother Lisa believed it to be an inconsequential necessity. Lisa died without ever knowing that her choice to tell Nico she had aborted their child, would cause the sort of chaos no one could've predicted or been prepared for. And so the butterfly effect begins.

"Grandma, you said you would give me the money so I can get my cheerleader uniform," Angel said when she walked in the kitchen and sat down at the table.

"I know and I will, baby. It's just taking grandma a little longer than I thought it would."

"Why is that?" Angel huffed.

"I had no idea with the cost of the uniform, shoes, practice gear and other stuff you would need almost $400. It's middle school for heavens sake. I didn't think it would be so expensive."

"But the only reason I even tried out for the squad was because you told me to. Now you don't even have the money for me to join."

"Angel, I told you to tryout because I knew you would make it. I use to see you outside practicing with Taren and you was way better than her and she was co-captain of the team. You would never admit it, but I knew you wanted to tryout. I just gave you the push you needed."

"Maybe, but like I said, what's the point of making the team if I can't join," Angel complained, playing with a napkin.

"Baby girl, don't grandma always come through for you? I told you, I'ma get the money. Have a little faith. Now eat yo' dinner. Wanna keep your weight right so you look cute in your uniform," her grandma teased, putting a hot plate of food on the table for Angel.

Angel smiled back at her grandmother with nothing but love in her eyes. Since the day she was born, her Grandma Eileen was all Angel had. Never knowing her mother or father, Angel's grandmother was her world and vice versa. Although Angel did want to join the cheerleading team it hurt her to heart to see her grandmother struggling to find a way to come up with the money she needed, but that was the story of their lives. Her grandmother worked two sometimes three jobs to make ends meet. They were always just getting by and often not even that. Angel could remember several occasions when the lights had been cut off or her grandmother barely had enough money to put gas in her car to get to work.

Through all the hard times, Angel never remembered her grandmother complaining once. That's why even though she loved practicing with her best friend Taren, she never had any intentions of trying out for the squad because she knew they couldn't afford it, but her grandmother insisted. Now Angel felt guilty that her grandmother was probably begging God for some sort of miracle to come up with the $400 she needed.

"Girl, I'm so excited we're going to be on the cheerleading squad together this year!" Taren beamed, as she sat in front of the mirror brushing her hair and making sexy faces. "Mica and the other girls are cool, but it's nothing like having your best friend to cheer at the games with," Taren continued, oblivious that Angel's mind somewhere else. "Angel, aren't you excited? All the football and basketball players are going to be checking for us. The girls are going to be so jelly!"

Angel was lying on Taren's bed staring up at the ceiling, not paying her friend any attention.

"Angel, are you listening to me?" Taren barked, as she stopped brushing her hair and turned to stare at her friend.

"Ummm, yeah, listening," Angel replied.

"Then what did I say?" Taren smacked, not believing her.

"Honestly, my mind is somewhere else, Taren," Angel admitted.

"Where else could your mind be... I mean what's more important than cheerleading? I mean besides clothes, shoes, makeup and of course Bryce Addison," Taren smiled, referring to her junior high boy crush.

"I don't think I'll be able to do cheerleading," Angel said sadly.

"What are talking about, you already made the team."

"Yeah, but my grandmother doesn't have the money to pay for my uniform and other stuff I'll need."

"Are you serious! What a bummer. There has to be a way," Taren said.

"She said that she would get it, but money is already tight. I feel bad that she even has to stress herself over it."

"Maybe I can ask my dad to give you the money," Taren suggested.

"No way!"

"Why not? You know he has the money. His car dealership business is doing extremely well. Look at this new iPod he just got me," Taren bragged, holding up the sleek blue gadget.

"I'm sure he does but I wouldn't feel right having you go to your father for me, plus my grandmother would have a fit. She always tells me not to accept handouts from anybody. That it's better to be without than to beg and if you want something work for it."

"Please, my mother asks for anything and everything she wants, that's why we don't go without nothing," Taren boasted.

"You're just lucky. You have both your parents. If I had a father with money, who I could just call and ask for anything I wanted, my life would be so much different. But it's just my grandmother and me. Even though we're poor, I still feel lucky to have her. I can't lie, I would love to have a rich father," Angel said.

Angel was always envious that Taren had both her mother and father in her life because she had neither. Even though Taren's parents didn't live together, her father always seemed to provide her with everything she wanted and needed.

Both girls lived in Sunrise, Florida, which was about 40 minutes away from Miami. Taren wasn't rich, but she lived with her mother in a nice townhouse on NW 125th Street, whereas Angel grew up in a small two-bedroom apartment on Sunrise Lakes Blvd in a somewhat rundown neighborhood. They had been best friends since elementary school, but as they were getting older, it was becoming more difficult for Angel to deal with Taren having it all and her having nothing.

"Wait! I have an idea," Taren said with excitement, lying on the bed next to Angel.

"What is it?"

"You know Malinda."

"Yeah, what about her, how can she help?" Angel questioned.

"Well, about a month ago she came to me asking did I want to earn some extra money. Like a few hundred dollars every week but I had to turn her down."

"A few hundred dollars?!" Angel repeated as her eyes widened. "Doing what?"

"All I would have to do was drop off and pick up a package twice a week."

"Are you crazy! Why did you turn her down?"

"Because the drop offs and pickups were on the other side of town. It's closer to where you live and I didn't feel like taking the bus over there twice a week. I mean it's not like I really need the money." Taren shrugged. "But it might be something you can do."

"You think so?" Angel asked, rising up from the bed.

"I don't know if Malinda still needs somebody to do it, but I'll call her now. It's worth a try," Taren said, reaching for her cell phone.

Angel stood up and began pacing the floor in Taren's bedroom. Her mind began racing thinking about how she would be able to buy everything she needed to join the cheerleading squad and take that burden off her grandmother. For the first time, Angel felt that maybe she would have an opportunity to have some sort of control of her destiny instead of always feeling hopeless.

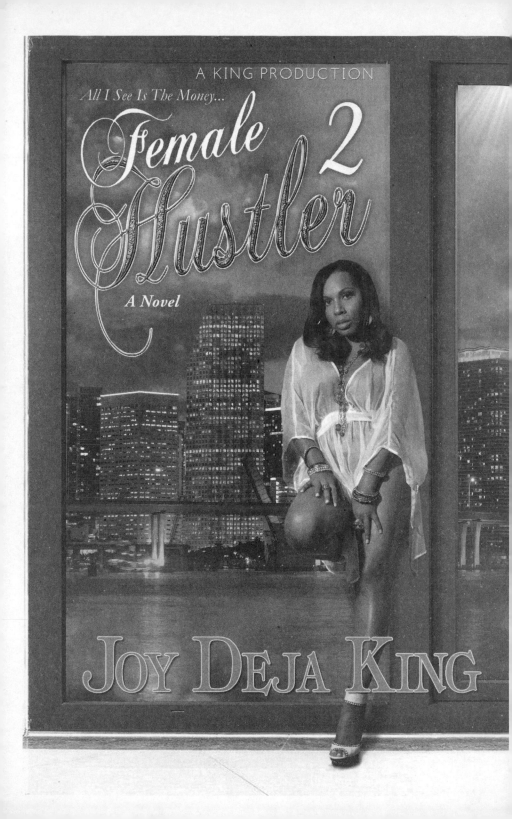

A KING PRODUCTION

Power

NO ONE MAN SHOULD HAVE ALL THAT POWER...BUT THERE WERE TWO

JOY DEJA KING

Chapter 1

UNDERGROUND KING

Alex stepped into his attorney's office to discuss what was always his number one priority...business. When he sat down their eyes locked and there was complete silence for the first few seconds. This was Alex's way of setting the tone of the meeting. His silence spoke volumes. This might've been his attorney's office but he was the head nigga in charge and nothing got started until he decided it was time to speak. Alex felt this approach was necessary. You see, after all these years of them doing business, attorney George Lofton still wasn't used to dealing with a man like Alex; a dirt-poor kid who could've easily died in the projects he was born in, but instead had made millions. It wasn't done the ski mask way but it was still illegal.

They'd first met when Alex was a sixteen-year-old kid growing up in TechWood Homes, a housing project in Atlanta. Alex and his best friend, Deion, had been arrested because the principal found 32 crack vials in Alex's book bag. Another kid had tipped the principal off and the principal subsequently called the police. Alex and Deion were arrested and suspended from school. His mother called George, who had the charges against them dismissed, and they were allowed to go back to school. But that wasn't the last time he would use George. He was arrested at twenty-two for attempted murder, and for trafficking cocaine a year later. Alex was acquitted on both charges. George Lofton later became known as the best trial attorney in Atlanta, but Alex had also become the best at what he did. And since it was Alex's money that kept Mr. Lofton in designer suits, million dollar homes and foreign cars, he believed he called the shots, and dared his attorney to tell him otherwise.

Alex noticed that what seemed like a long period of silence made Mr. Lofton feel uncomfortable, which he liked. Out of habit, in order to camouflage the discomfort, his attorney always kept bottled water within arm's reach. He would cough, take a swig, and lean back in his chair, raising his eyebrows a little, trying to give a look of certainty, though he wasn't completely confident at all in Alex's presence. The reason was because Alex did what many had thought would be impossible, especially men like George Lofton. He had gone from a knucklehead, low-level drug dealer to an underground king and an unstoppable respected criminal boss.

Before finally speaking, Alex gave an intense stare into George Lofton's piercing eyes. They were not only the bluest he had ever seen, but also some of the most calculating. The latter is what Alex found so compelling. A calculating attorney working on his behalf could almost guarantee a get out of jail free card for the duration of his criminal career.

"Have you thought over what we briefly discussed the other day?" Alex asked his attorney, finally breaking the silence.

"Yes I have, but I want to make sure I understand you correctly. You want to give me six hundred thousand to represent you or your friend Deion if you are ever arrested and have to stand trial again in the future?"

Alex assumed he had already made himself clear based on their previous conversations and was annoyed by what he now considered a repetitive question. "George, you know I don't like repeating myself. That's exactly what I'm saying. Are we clear?"

"So this is an unofficial retainer."

"Yes, you can call it that."

George stood and closed the blinds then walked over to the door that led to the reception area. He turned the deadbolt so they wouldn't be disturbed. George sat back behind the desk. "You know that if you and your friend Deion are ever on the same case that I can't represent the both of you."

"I know that."

"So what do you propose I do if that was ever to happen?"

"You would get him the next best attorney in Atlanta," Alex said without hesitation. Deion was Alex's best friend—had been since the first grade. They were now business partners, but the core of their bond was built on that friendship, and because of that Alex would always look out for Deion's best interest.

"That's all I need to know."

Alex clasped his hands and stared at the ceiling for a moment, thinking that maybe it was a bad idea bringing the money to George. Maybe he should have just put it somewhere safe only known to him and his mom. He quickly dismissed his concerns.

"Okay. Where's the money?" Alex presented George with two leather briefcases. He opened the first one and was glad to see that it was all hundred-dollar bills. When he closed the briefcase he asked, "There is no need to count this is there?"

"You can count it if you want, but it's all there."

George took another swig of water. The cash made him nervous. He planned to take it directly to one of his bank safe deposit boxes. The two men stood. Alex was a foot taller than George; he had flawless mahogany skin, a deep brown with a bit of a red tint, broad shoulders, very large hands, and a goatee. He was a man's man. With such a powerful physical appearance, Alex kept his style very low-key. His only display of wealth was a pricey diamond watch that his best friend and partner Deion had bought him for his birthday.

"I'll take good care of this, and you," his attorney said, extending his hand to Alex.

"With this type of money, I know you will," Alex stated without flinching. Alex gave one last lingering stare into his attorney's piercing eyes. "We do have a clear understanding...correct?"

"Of course. I've never let you down and I never will. That, I promise you." The men shook hands and

Alex made his exit with the same coolness as his entrance.

With Alex embarking on a new, potentially dangerous business venture, he wanted to make sure that he had all his bases covered. The higher up he seemed to go on the totem pole, the costlier his problems became. But Alex welcomed new challenges because he had no intention of ever being a nickel and dime nigga again.

A KING PRODUCTION

Power 2

NO ONE MAN SHOULD HAVE ALL THAT POWER...BUT THERE WERE TWO

JOY DEJA KING

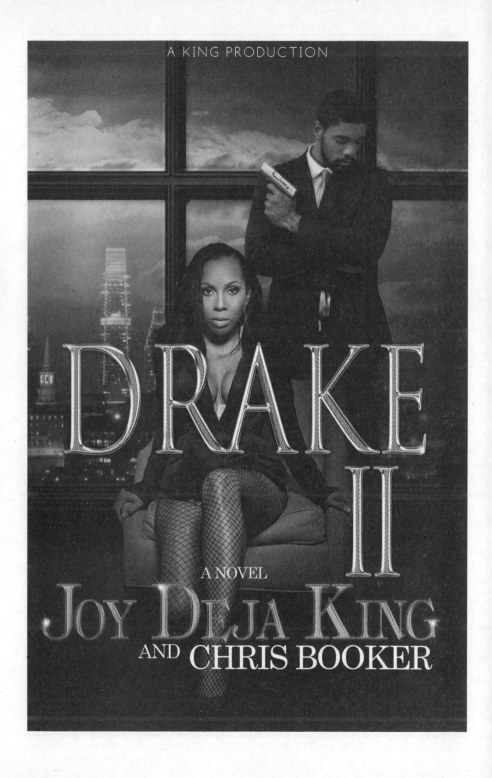

A KING PRODUCTION

DRAKE II

A NOVEL

JOY DEJA KING
AND CHRIS BOOKER